Let Us Prey

Gerald Hammond

St. Martin's Press
New York

Library of Congress Cataloging-in-Publication Data

Hammond, Gerald.
    Let us prey / Gerald Hammond.
        p.   cm.
    ISBN 0-312-05891-8
    I. Title.
    PR6058.A55456L4   1991
    823'.914—dc20   90-27898
                                                                                              CIP

First published in Great Britain by Macmillan London Limited.

First U.S. Edition: August 1991
10 9 8 7 6 5 4 3 2 1

Let Us Prey

ONE

From my office window I could look across the Square of Newton Lauder. Ill-named though it was, being a rather lop-sided triangle, it was a pleasing prospect. From my viewpoint the modern tower of the police building, clean-lined and efficient but quite unsuited to a small country town in the Scottish Borders, was almost hidden behind the hotel and the other buildings which had been constructed in a more gracious age.

The good weather which we often experience in early summer, but which rarely lasts after the longest day, was holding. The small trees in the Square and the larger species peering over the rooftops had not long before burst into leaf and their green still had the freshness of any young thing. The smaller trees hid most of the tin boxes which cluttered the Square. If I half closed my eyes I could imagine the scene as it had been a hundred years earlier, without having to suffer the noise of hoofs and iron-shod wheels or the inconveniences imposed by the needs of the horses. (Not, I must emphasise, that I had been in legal practise in the town for quite so long as that; but in the many years, more than I would care to admit, that I had overlooked the Square from the same office I had witnessed the final demise of the horse and trap.)

The imperative note of the telephone jerked me out

7

of what had become a light doze. I rotated my chair and picked up the receiver. I dislike listening to disembodied voices, much preferring to watch the eyes and hands of the speaker, but needs must in a modern age.

'Mr Enterkin?' my secretary/receptionist enquired politely. She always made the enquiry, in case I had mysteriously vanished and my phone was being answered by the window-cleaner.

I confirmed, for the ten-thousandth time, that I was indeed myself.

'Sir Peter wants a word with you.'

Miss Jelks put Sir Peter Hay through to me. I was always glad to hear from him. He was a good friend and, being the largest landowner for some miles around, was a regular source of quite profitable business.

'Ralph,' he said. His voice, especially over the telephone, always made my name sound like the yapping of a small dog. 'Are you busy just now?'

As it happened, I had cleared my desk of several conveyances of property and a request for counsel's opinion on the meaning of some words in a Victorian trust deed. I had been looking forward to a period of peace and pottering, but it does not do to seem under-occupied. 'Not excessively,' I said.

'Good, good,' he said. 'You know Alec Deeley at Ladyhill Woods?'

'By name only.'

'Likely so. He keeps himself to himself and stays out of trouble – until now. His keeper's been found dead. No suspicion of foul play as far as I'm aware, unless you count the poisoning of birds of prey, but there seems to be trouble brewing. He phoned, asking me to recommend a solicitor. Of course I thought of you. Can you get out there straight away and find out what really happened?'

'Not very easily,' I said. Greatly though I admire

8

the scenery of the Scottish Borders, I prefer to admire it from afar rather than to go wandering around its manifold discomforts, seeking directions from passers-by who, if they know the way to my destination, are quite incapable of conveying clear instructions to anyone not already conversant with the route. Even less does my admiration extend to walking through it. My joints are no longer as supple as once they were, nor am I quite so slim. 'Couldn't he come to me?' I suggested.

'The police are making themselves obnoxious,' Sir Peter said. 'They may have left by now but they'll certainly be back. And Alec says that their version of events is not possible. Go and see him, there's a good chap. Look into it thoroughly.'

Those few gentle words glossed over a direct order to a solicitor from his largest client. 'He might be better with somebody else,' I said uneasily. 'You know that I'm not an investigator. And I'm out of my depth when it comes to fieldsports and guns and things.'

'Nonsense,' he said briskly. 'You've pulled off more than one coup.'

'The credit for which must go to Keith Calder.'

'Take him along with you. Alec can afford a fee for Keith's services. Or, if he can't, we can work something out. Keith owes me several favours.'

'Keith was at the shop earlier,' I said, 'but I saw him drive off.'

'If you've time to keep looking out of the window, you can't be so busy,' he said triumphantly. 'I'll see if I can't track him down and ask him to catch up with you. Cheerio. No time to waste.' And before I could protest that I was awaiting an urgent phone-call from Australia, or possibly the moon, he had disconnected.

Miss Jelks, who had undoubtedly been listening to

our discussion, opened my door. 'When will you be back?' she asked.

'God knows,' I said gloomily.

'If a client calls . . . ?'

'Tell them I'm dead.' (She nodded, knowing better than to take me literally.) 'See if you can catch my wife on the phone.'

Some years before, I had startled the local community by marrying a barmaid. But she had also been a farmer's widow, steeped in the lore of the countryside. I had never verified the fact for myself but I had been assured that she was also a competent shot. Her advice might be almost as good as Keith's and would certainly be more restful.

The phone burped at me again and Penny was on the line. 'Miss Jelks caught me as I was going out of the door,' she said.

'To the hotel?' I asked.

'Of course.'

I had never objected to Penny resuming her career, part time. Some of my legal confrères had considered it infra dig. that I should have a wife serving behind the bar of Newton Lauder's premier hotel, although as the years went by they had come to accept it as one of the more eccentric facts of life, but the information which she sometimes gathered in that hotbed of gossip far outweighed any social stigma. If a usually open-handed drinker started avoiding company which would entail large rounds, he might not be worthy of the loan which he was trying to negotiate; while if there were to be a serious flaw in the case which some local worthy was bringing against one of my clients it would certainly be whispered in the bar and Penny, as much a part of the furnishings as the bottles and beer-handles, would hear it.

'Can you get off?' I asked. 'I need your help.'

10

'I expect so,' she said. 'I've stood in for Lucy twice recently. She owes me.'

I arranged to meet her in the Square.

Among the tin boxes which cluttered the Square was one which, I liked to think, stood out as having been built by craftsmen rather than stamped out of cheap tinware. This was my old Rover. It might, like its owner, be somewhat tired and even a little rusty but it resembled me also in being sturdy, old-fashioned and dignified, if perhaps at times a little greedy.

I unlocked the car and wound down a couple of windows to let the stale air escape. There was still no sign of Penny. The Rover was parked just opposite the gunshop so I walked across and looked inside.

Janet James, the wife of Keith Calder's partner, seemed to be in sole charge for the moment. 'Sir Peter already phoned,' she said before I could speak. 'I told him that Keith had just picked up two guns for servicing.'

'He'll be at home, then?' (Keith lived about two miles to the north of the town, at Briesland House, and his workshop was there.)

'Eventually,' Janet said. 'If he doesn't spot a friend or a field of pigeon by the wayside. Don't let him get involved for more than a day or two. Guns are coming in for out-of-season servicing and we're getting enquiries about coaching from the summer visitors. What drama's going on this time?'

'No drama. There's been an accident,' I said. 'That's all I know. I've probably only been invoked to fend off compensation claims or a prosecution under the Health and Safety at Work Act.'

'Not if Sir Peter's looking for Keith,' Janet said. 'If Keith gets involved, there will be drama.'

I walked thoughtfully back to the Rover. There was some truth in her words. Keith Calder had set up a gunshop in the Square and over the years he and Wallace James had built it up into a thriving business. In addition to retailing all the expensive gadgetry which the fieldsportsman seems to find necessary and servicing, repairing and altering firearms, they had become noted dealers in antique guns. Outwith the strict confines of the business, however, Keith's curiosity and his knowledge, combined, had led him to investigate a series of crimes involving firearms – with such success that he was often persuaded to act as consultant by one side or the other.

I had seated myself at the passenger's side of the car. My musing was interrupted by the arrival of Penny. Knowing my distrust of mechanical contrivances, even the Rover, she lowered her deliciously plump backside into the driver's east.

'I'm wanted from five o'clock,' she said. 'Until then, I'm free. Where are we going?'

'Ladyhill Woods,' I said. 'Alexander Deeley's place. It's somewhere in the hinterland to the east.'

'I know where it is.' She backed the car out and set off round the corner of the Town Hall, climbing the hill to the canal bridge. 'What are we going to do out there?'

'We'll find out when we get there,' I told her. 'All I know at the moment is that Mr Deeley's gamekeeper seems to have met with a fatal accident. The ways of the sporting fraternity are a closed book to me, so I asked for your companionship. Keith may show his face but his advice is usually incomprehensible. I need an interpreter. We might have lunch at Whisbeck Grange on the way home,' I added.

Penny made an approving noise. She enjoys a good meal as much as I do. 'We could stop and make a booking.'

12

'Better not,' I said. 'We don't know how long we'll be.'
We picked our way through a network of small roads and crossed a stretch of moorland. 'If it's Jim Broxburn who's had the accident,' Penny said suddenly, 'I wouldn't have called him Mr Deeley's gamekeeper.'

'What would you have called him, then?' I asked.

'Not what,' she said obscurely. 'Whose. What I mean is, he didn't just work for Mr Deeley. He worked the night-shift at the bakery but he did some part-time keepering. Mr Deeley owns Ladyhill Farm although he has a manager to run the place. He put together the sporting rights to two or three adjoining farms and formed a syndicate. Mr Deeley's the secretary and chairman, but all the same it was the syndicate that Jim worked for. It's a very low-key thing, not one of your big shoots.'

'To me,' I said, 'a shoot is a shoot.'

'Just as a car is a car, whether it's a rusty Mini or a new Rolls?'

'Is there that much difference?' I asked.

Her voice took on the 'Are you sitting comfortably?' tone which she usually adopts when I am being particularly ignorant about matters rural. 'At the top end of the market you may have eight Guns being served by twenty beaters and several keepers and pickers-up. Many of those shoots have had to go at least partly commercial and take paying Guns at so much per bird.

'At Ladyhill Woods you have a few friends with at the most a part-time keeper but doing much of the work themselves. They walk their birds up or they split into two groups and beat for each other; they don't hire beaters unless they're expecting a very poor turnout, and even then they mostly make do with friends and relatives.'

'How do you know all this?' I asked. Her omniscience never ceased to amaze me.

'Jim used to come into the bar with one or two of

13

the members on shoot days. And I went to beat for them once, when they were expecting an elderly guest and there was flu among the syndicate members. It was while you were away. Larry Crawford asked me to and I owed him a favour. He's a member.'

I found myself nodding. There was always an explanation for what I would otherwise have put down to witchcraft. 'What can you tell me about Jim Broxburn?' I asked.

She drove in silence for a mile or two while she thought about it. 'Single,' she said at last. 'Thirtyish. Average height but sturdily built. Dark with craggy sort of features. Very outspoken – he thought nothing of telling you to piss off, in so many words, whether you were a pauper or a politician. And yet . . . ' She fell silent again.

'And yet?' I said.

'It's difficult to put into words. He was strong-minded and argumentative. I've heard him get into a slanging match in the bar at least ten times. But his side of the argument was always ethical, if that's the word I want. I don't think that he attended church, but he seemed to be a man of conscience. He had intense, personal ideas of right and wrong.'

'Not a comfortable person to have around,' I suggested.

'Not if you didn't happen to agree with him,' Penny said. 'Yet most folk seemed to like him and those who didn't were the ones I wouldn't want to know.'

And that, I thought, was praise indeed. 'Do you know as much about Alexander Deeley?' I asked.

'Very little,' she said. 'A retired tea-planter, I think, or something like that. I've only met him once but I liked him.'

Our road followed the line where high moorland gives way to the fertile plain which runs to the Border. Twenty

14

minutes from Newton Lauder we came to the brink of a valley with a wide and undulating floor and a sudden change of scenery. Open moorland gave way to fields, green but with startling splashes of yellow which Penny said was rape, although to the lawyer the word has quite a different connotation. Instead of wire fences, the fields were divided by hedgerows punctuated by tall trees.

'Very attractive,' I said.

'It's not what you'd call prairie farming,' Penny said. 'It's been farmed for the shooting. Not very economical. I'm surprised that they haven't claimed a grant for tearing out the hedges and another grant to plant them again.'

The view of the fields was broken by trees. It was as though irregular balls of leaf had blown across the moors until caught by the valley. It was cosy scenery, not out of keeping with the Borders but oddly set in the midst of moorland. I decided that the valley made a sheltered microclimate.

The car eased cautiously down a steep and narrow road and then took to the level between high hedges. Penny, who has a much better sense of direction and memory for roads than I will ever have, hesitated once at a junction and then eased the car through a pair of gates and up a driveway which was a dark tunnel under trees which met overhead. We emerged on to a sunlit sweep of gravel in front of a house. The difference between a substantial farmhouse and one which has been built as a small Gentleman's Residence is not always marked. From the plain and informal style of the place and the loom of a barn through a gap in the trees I judged that this had been built as a farmhouse, but the spacious garden suggested that it had passed into the other use years earlier. A pair of Labradors on the doorstep raised their heads but otherwise ignored us.

The only shade to fall from a towering tree and across

15

the gravel was already occupied by a small car of a colour which I usually associate with the dung of unhealthy animals. Penny pulled up in the sun.

Across the gravel from the house was an irregular expanse of well-mown lawn fringed with shrubs in flower. A white table had been placed in the shade of the same large tree and seated at it, on two of the several white garden chairs, were two men. As I got out of the car they both rose and the elder of them walked to meet me.

He must have been in his sixties although he moved like a much younger man. I envied him that much, although his easy stride had been bought at the expense of a narrow waist. Either he had been blessed with an ideal metabolism or cursed with poor appetite. His hair, if he had any, was hidden by a panama hat on what seemed to be a long head but his sideburns were white. His face was lined and had the sallowness of skin which has been kept for too long in hot climes, but the underlying features were firm yet friendly and faintly patrician. He was dressed for comfort, in slacks, sandals and a T-shirt but there was no mistaking him for the gardener.

'Mr Enterkin?' he said. 'Peter Hay said that you were on your way. Good of you to drop everything and come so promptly.' His voice was accentless – it would have been called 'BBC' before the Beeb decided that regional accents were 'in'.

He led me to the table under the tree. Down in the valley we seemed to have lost what breeze had been alleviating the unusual heat and sweat was moistening my collar, but under the tree it was cool.

The other man had stood waiting. He wore an off-the-peg suit but had loosened his tie as a small concession to the heat. He looked young to me, as does anybody under thirty. He was tall but not heavy, with a bullet head neatly cropped and a plain face which struck me as dogged

16

rather than intelligent. His expression was meant to be neutral but I was warned by something in his attitude which reminded me of a cat preparing to pounce.

'This is Sergeant Fuller,' Mr Deeley said. (The Sergeant and I exchanged nods.) 'I understood that Mr Calder was coming with you.' His tone suggested that Keith's absence was more of a loss than mine would have been.

'He seems to have gone off somewhere,' I said. 'He'll probably follow me up when Sir Peter's messages catch up with him. In the meantime I brought my wife along as my adviser on matters of keepering and country lore, but she preferred to wait in the car until needed.'

'No need for that,' Mr Deeley said. 'You two sit down.' He set off towards the car and I saw him stoop and speak to Penny. The Sergeant and I took chairs and exchanged a few stilted remarks. He had an open notebook before him but evidently my comments on the heat of the day were not judged worth recording for posterity. I saw Penny get out of the car and go into the house.

'Mrs Enterkin will be with us in a minute,' Mr Deeley said, rejoining us and taking a seat in his original chair. 'Now let me tell you what's happened.'

'I'd rather hear it from the Sergeant,' I said.

A faint frown shadowed Mr Deeley's eyes. 'Surely my version is what should matter to you.'

'It does,' I said. 'Very much. But I'd prefer to hear the Sergeant, if you don't mind – firstly because what he's gathered from you and others may be fuller and more relevant than your limited view and, secondly, because in the light of what the Sergeant says I may want to speak with you in private before advising you. Remember that I know nothing as yet.'

'I understand,' Mr Deeley said.

The Sergeant looked uncomfortable. Nobody had coached him on how to react to a solicitor who was

17

determined to dictate the course of an interview. 'I can give you certain facts,' he said at last.

I was about to tell him, quite kindly, to get on with it. But I was not yet to be put in the picture. Penny came out of the house carrying a tray with glasses and a large jug which proved to contain iced lemonade. She greeted Sergeant Fuller by name, which suggested that he was not unknown in the bar of the hotel. 'Your wife asked me whether we'd be staying to lunch,' she told Mr Deeley. 'I said that I'd no idea how long we'd be here and she said that it would only be cold meat and salad so we could let her know later. I hope that's all right?' she added to me.

I made up my mind to conduct my business and depart as quickly as was consistent with my client's interests. Even in such heat, lunch at Whisbeck Grange was to be preferred to cold meat and salad in a stranger's house. 'We'll see,' I said. 'The Sergeant was about to give us the story.'

Sergeant Fuller had accepted a glass of lemonade. He took a sip, first sniffing to make sure that nothing alcoholic had been slipped into it.

'A call was received by the local police at three minutes past eight this morning. It was from a Mrs Chegwin.'

Mr Deeley seemed about to interrupt but I frowned him down. 'Mrs Chegwin?' I said to Penny.

As I expected, my wife knew of Mrs Chegwin. 'Yes. She's a prominent local lady, a pillar of the National Trust and the Royal Society for the Protection of Birds. Her photographs of birds win prizes. She's a staunch protectionist.'

'That's so,' said the Sergeant. 'In fact, our man was at first led to believe that she was complaining about an infringement of the Wildlife and Countryside Act and it was several minutes before she got around to mentioning a dead body. As soon as it was made clear that there had been a fatality, the local man notified HQ and then attended here. A team from HQ arrived almost on his heels.'

The Sergeant consulted his notes. 'At a point known locally as Gled Corner, a dead man was found. Mr Deeley was informed and he identified the man as his part-time keeper, James Broxburn.'

Penny gave me a warning glance but I had already decided to intervene. Mr Deeley might be prepared to let the point go, but small errors can sometimes prove crucial if they are allowed to get into the record. 'As I understand it,' I said, 'Mr Broxburn was not Mr Deeley's employee but was employed by the syndicate.'

The Sergeant looked both surprised and vexed. 'That isn't what Mr Deeley led us to believe.'

'You may as well explain,' I told Mr Deeley.

He shrugged. 'I don't think that I led you to believe anything in particular. It seemed unimportant. He was usually referred to as my keeper. In point of fact, it's a moot point whether he was employed here at all. He was paid no wages and his cards were stamped by the bakery. In his spare time he looked after the keepering here in return for a free half-gun in the syndicate and a rent-free cottage.'

'Half-gun?' said the Sergeant, writing busily.

'That means that he could shoot as a member of the syndicate on half the occasions in the year.'

'Now that that's cleared up,' I said, 'we can move on.'

The Sergeant finished writing. 'The police surgeon confirmed death and gave a tentative opinion that the man had died between six and seven; that is, between one and two hours before the finding of his body by Mrs Chegwin.

'The body was lying on its face. Beside the right hand

19

was a hypodermic syringe. The left hand still gripped the body of a small bird which one of our officers stated was a pheasant chick. Or poult,' the Sergeant added. The terminology seemed to be as confusing to him as it was to me. 'A small bottle stood on the ground nearby containing a blue liquid.

'The body . . . ' The Sergeant paused and pulled a face indicative of distaste. He looked, for a moment, rather more human and distinctly less hostile. 'It turned me up, I don't mind telling you. It was the opinion of the police surgeon, subject to post-mortem examination, that a powerful poison was involved, possibly – ' the Sergeant paused, consulted his notes and took a deep breath ' – a non-barbiturate irritant and respiratory depressant such as chloral hydrate. There was a small wound between the thumb and first finger of the left hand.

'Mr Deeley assured us that we were welcome to search the area and premises. Adjoining Mr Deeley's house there is an outbuilding, possibly a former wash-house, which Mr Deeley told us had been used by Mr Broxburn as a store in connection with his keepering. In it we found a tin containing capsules of blue powder. According to the manufacturer's printing, the capsules are put down for rats. The rats eat their way into the capsules, which contain – ' the Sergeant again consulted his notes ' – alpha-chloralose. According to the police surgeon, alpha-chloralose is metabolised into chloral hydrate in the body. Those are the facts.' The Sergeant snapped his notebook shut and met my eye in silence. In his own eye was a faint gleam of triumph. 'Get out of that,' he seemed to be saying.

Those might be the facts, but there were many inferences. If foul play were suspected, the area would be alive with policemen and Mr Deeley would be being questioned more formally and by more senior officers. Yet both

Alexander Deeley and Penny were looking worried. I remembered one of Sir Peter's comments; and although the provisions of the Wildlife and Countryside Act 1981 were far from fresh in my mind I began to share their anxiety.

'So the body was removed and your superiors went back to Headquarters,' I said.

The Sergeant agreed.

'Leaving you behind to ask Mr Deeley what questions?'

'I asked Mr Deeley whether he knew about the material in the outbuilding. He replied that the material had been bought on his instructions because there had been an outbreak of rats on the shoot. When you arrived, I was about to ask him what instructions he had given Mr Broxburn about the control of predators.'

Silence came down again, except for the song of a bird in the tree above us. All three were waiting for me to say something brilliant and my mind had come to the end of its understanding. 'Go for a short walk, Sergeant,' I said. 'I'll confer with Mr Deeley and decide for myself whether he should answer you.'

The Sergeant got to his feet. His expression left me in no doubt that he would have been better pleased if some accident had delayed my arrival until later, if at all. But that, after all, is the natural relationship between defence solicitors and the police. I blessed Sir Peter for the urgency on which he had insisted.

When he was out of earshot, I said, 'What exactly do they suspect?'

'It seems clear enough,' Deeley said. 'They think that he was putting out poisoned bait for a raptor.'

'Birds of prey,' Penny murmured. 'Hawks, falcons and eagles. And owls. Highly illegal.'

'Couldn't he have been baiting for rats?' I asked.

'He wouldn't have been injecting a carcass,' Deeley

said impatiently. 'Not for rats. You heard the Sergeant. The stuff comes in a capsule which rats eat into. Then goodbye rat. That way it's safe. But when a gamekeeper lays alpha-chloralose for a raptor – and it does happen sometimes, no matter what the law says – he cuts open the capsule and makes a solution. Anyway, I don't believe a word of it.'

'So what instructions did you give him?'

'None. It was never necessary. Personally, if he'd asked me I'd have had to tell him to take no action but I'd have been ambivalent about it.' Deeley shrugged and looked round for the Sergeant, but he was at the far end of the lawn, admiring an azalea bush ablaze with flowers. 'Buzzards and sparrowhawks are protected by law but they're a long way from being endangered. Usually they don't do much harm; in fact they often do good by controlling rodents and crows, but if a sparrowhawk once starts taking your pheasant poults to feed her chicks she tends to come back every day. It's asking a lot of a keeper who takes a pride in his job to stand by and watch his stock being taken four or five months before the season starts.

'But Jimmy Broxburn cared as much for the rest of wildlife as he did for his pheasants. And he was very law-abiding. Once, several years ago, we had a shoot on the very last day of the pheasant season and he gave one of the members a roasting for lifting his gun to a woodcock. Well, we don't see many woodcock around here, so the members can get excited when they turn up.'

Penny saw that I was out of my depth again. 'The pheasant season ends on the first of February,' she said. 'But woodcock go out of season on the thirty-first of January. It's crazy but it's the law.'

'I could give you a dozen examples,' Deeley said.

'But, believe me, Jim would never have set poison for a hawk.'

'But if he had,' I said. 'Off the cuff and without having had time to look up recent cases, I would expect his employer to be charged with "causing or permitting".'

He looked grim. 'The employer's sometimes prosecuted if it can be proved that the keeper was working to his instructions. There was a case not long ago. And that damned Chegwin woman has been niggling away at the police – otherwise, frankly, they'd probably have written it off as an unfortunate accident. She kept repeating that an offence had been committed; and she was adamant that Jim was working under my orders.'

'But he wasn't,' I said. It was half a question.

'No.'

'Does she have anything which might seem to support her allegation?'

'Not that I know of. I suppose the fact that the stuff was in a store which forms part of my house makes it look bad.'

'Bad,' I said, 'but not disastrous. Here's the Sergeant coming back. My wife and I will withdraw. Tell him what you've told me – that you don't believe that Broxburn would poison – what did you call them? – raptors and that you never gave him any instructions on the subject. Tell him that and nothing more. And I wouldn't be too outspoken about your personal views,' I added. I got to my feet and held out a hand to Penny.

Deeley showed surprise. 'Don't you want to be present?' he asked.

'If I'm present, he can ask more questions,' I pointed out. 'If not, you have an excuse not to answer. Anyway, I hear the unmistakable sound of Keith Calder's jeep approaching.'

TWO

The strange little Japanese vehicle, like a Land-rover shrunk in the wash, which Keith used as his personal and shooting vehicle, emerged from the tunnel of trees and stopped beside us on the gravel. The back of it was entirely taken up by space for dogs – two were in evidence – and storage for guns, decoys, camouflage nets and assorted gear which I could not have put a name to, so Penny got into the passenger seat while I leaned uncomfortably to talk through the open window.

'I brought Penny along to advise me, in your absence,' I explained.

'You couldn't have done better,' Keith said with apparent sincerity.

It took me only a minute or two to summarise the developments for Keith, even though I was being helped and occasionally corrected on minor details by Penny. Keith listened intently, staring through the windscreen to where the discussion between Mr Deeley and Sergeant Fuller was proceeding from wary co-operation towards visible acrimony.

When we had finished, he sat thinking for a few more seconds. 'Could you find out what the dead man had in his pockets?' he asked suddenly.

'I could try,' I said.

'Better hurry. The fuzz is about to take off.'

25

I looked up. The two men had walked to the Sergeant's car. I hurried to join them and asked the question. The Sergeant looked at me coldly. 'In view of Mr Deeley's attitude,' he said, 'I think I should ask you to obtain your information through the proper channels. Nothing can be decided until we have the forensic report, but if the autopsy and the analyses show what one would expect there will be no avoiding certain questions.'

I looked at Deeley. 'Did Mr Broxburn have a wife or any near relatives?' I asked him.

'No wife. A sister in Canada. I don't know of any others.'

'Then it would be reasonable for you to suggest my name as the proper person to administer his estate pending the appointment of an executor.'

Deeley caught on immediately. 'I was about to do so,' he said.

'What estate?' asked the Sergeant. 'The contents of the cottage – '

'And of his pockets,' I said.

Sergeant Fuller bit back what might have been a hot retort and sighed ostentatiously. He produced his notebook and read rapidly. I thanked him politely.

His car spurted past me as I walked back to the jeep.

Keith and Penny had left the little vehicle and I had to look up to Keith's face. Not that he is particularly tall, but if I have been gifted with inches it is not in the vertical direction. 'Handkerchief,' I told him. 'Some coins. A letter from Canada. Knife. Matches. Wallet with three fivers, two pound notes and some old receipts. A wad of toilet paper. Half a bar of chocolate and some indigestion tablets. He was wearing a cartridge belt.'

Keith looked at me in silence for a few seconds. My client joined us. 'Mr Calder,' he said. 'Thank you for coming. We've met before.'

'Of course,' Keith said. 'You've been coming into the shop for years. I put new springs into a rather good Churchill for you. As for coming . . . it was no trouble, over something potentially serious. I only hope that I can help. Could we go and see where it happened?'

'Certainly,' Deeley said. 'I think that the police have abandoned the area altogether. We could walk up there now.'

'What a good idea!' I said. 'But first, where did Mr Broxburn live?'

'In a cottage behind the house,' Deeley said. 'Why?'

'If I'm going to deal with his estate, I should have a look at his things,' I said vaguely. 'See what kind of mess the police have made. Look for his sister's address without waiting for the police to disgorge that letter. That sort of thing. Three people are more than enough for looking at the scene of a fatal accident.'

'Don't be so silly,' Penny said affectionately. 'A little stroll won't hurt you. The mention of the word "walk",' she explained to Mr Deeley, 'especially in the same sentence as "up", always brings out the sluggard in my husband.'

'It isn't buried very deep,' Keith added. 'May I bring my dogs?'

'Please do,' Mr Deeley said. 'I'll leave mine. My one dog, I mean. The other belonged to Jim Broxburn. He usually left him here while he went round his traps. The smell of a dog can act as a danger signal.' The two Labradors had risen, hoping for a walk, but at a word from Deeley they lay down again, watching us with sad eyes. 'Better to leave them here,' Deeley said. 'The scent where his master died . . . '

Keith let a spaniel and a black Labrador out of the jeep. The two pairs of dogs pretended to ignore each other.

We followed a farm track which seemed to climb steeply for miles, although the valley floor had seemed almost flat when we had looked down from the rim; and when I looked back I was surprised to see that the house and cars, which I had thought must be beneath the horizon, were still in view and not much below us.

We passed a small wood of mixed conifers and deciduous trees, tightly fenced against cattle. The track curled round the end. Beyond a broad field of grass which held a few halfwitted-looking sheep we saw a continuation of our original road and a house which had once been two cottages. The origin was evident, but the work had been well done with the addition of a garage, a picture window and a conservatory. A small garden, tucked between another field and another wood, was in full flower.

'Very pretty,' Penny said.

'And only woman is vile,' said Mr Deeley. His tone would have been more suited to the discussion of a social disease. 'That's where the awful Mrs Chegwin dwells, glaring out disapprovingly at almost everything anybody cares to do. I dare say that she's got the binoculars on us, but never mind. With a little luck, you need never meet her.'

We seemed to have come to a halt. I sat down thankfully on a half-tumbled section of dry-stone wall. My shirt was clinging to me.

'I already know her,' Keith said. 'I, of course, being a shooting man, am beneath her contempt; but she's a bit more open-minded about Molly. Because of their common interest in wildlife photography and her need to use Molly's darkroom from time to time she manages to overlook the fact that Molly sometimes shoots. She has her own set-up, but Molly's is far better equipped,' he said complacently.

'She has a similar problem with a falconer who lives

further up the valley,' Deeley said. 'You can just see the top of his building above the next rise. She loves him for preserving birds of prey and hates him because his hawks kill other birds. If they lived on cat food, that would be quite acceptable.

'Personally, I'd be glad to see the back of him. Last year, somebody brought him an eagle which had broken a wing against an overhead power cable. He nursed it back to health and was planning to release it back in its native Cromarty. But it got loose for a fortnight last season and our pheasants were scared to get off the ground. Jim swore that it was taking partridges. And I don't think he's above flying his hawks at our gamebirds.' He stopped and pulled a wry face. 'But I'm procrastinating. My subconscious insists that Jim will be lying where I last saw him.' He began to walk again, but the spring had gone out of his step. 'The place we want is just round the corner. It was always one of my favourite pegs on a shooting day but I don't think I could bring myself to stand there again.'

'These things pass,' Keith said.

Deeley led us off the track and through an open gate. A triangle of rough ground tapered down the side of the wood, ending at a fence beyond which another field held some cereal crop. Over a wide area the weeds had been trampled down. He led us to a barer circle carpeted with moss and wildflowers.

'This is where Jim was found,' he said.

We stood around with bowed heads. I wondered whether this was out of respect for the dead but from the cogitative noises which Penny and Keith were making I decided that the silence was for study and thought.

I had had time for some thinking of my own. 'Why did you say that the matter could be serious?' I asked Keith. 'At the worst, it should lead to no more than a modest fine . . . '

He looked up and ran his fingers through his hair. I had watched Keith progress over the years from a young man, amoral and rather wild, into a solid businessman who could usually (but not always) be trusted to behave with sense and discretion; but his black hair was still thick and only slightly streaked with grey and for the rest the handsome devil who had once both charmed and terrified the mothers of daughters had not been expunged by the depredations of age.

Keith was noticeably irritated by my interruption but nevertheless willing to answer stupid questions. 'A sheriff might decide that Jim Broxburn was getting moneysworth for his labour. That could make him an employee. If he also decided that Jim was acting on the orders of Mr Deeley as . . . chairman, is it?'

'And secretary,' Deeley said.

' – as chairman and secretary of the syndicate, Mr Deeley could be found guilty of an offence. I dare say that the syndicate would club together to pay the fine, but if the police are hostile they could well use it as an excuse to remove Mr Deeley's shotgun certificate.'

One gets used to thinking of legal penalties as comprising fines or imprisonment, any other sanctions being neither here nor there. I was on the point of asking whether such a loss would constitute the end of the world when I remembered how seriously these shooting men take any curtailment of their activities.

Keith grunted suddenly. 'I don't buy the police theory,' he said.

'Nor do I,' Penny said. 'For one thing, if he was setting bait he'd set it right where the last chick was taken. But I don't see even a single feather.'

'Well, I certainly don't believe it,' Deeley said. 'Jim Broxburn would never set poison for hawks. I've known him go without sleep to stand guard, as a sort of animated scarecrow, when he thought that his chicks might be in danger. Eventually, the buzzards decided that fieldmice made an easier meal.'

'Do you really have buzzards here?' I asked. I had seen it suggested on television that buzzards were becoming a great rarity.

'For God's sake use your eyes,' Keith said.

Penny pointed to where, in the distance, a large bird was circling. 'Why do you think they call this Gled Corner?' she asked.

'I haven't the faintest idea,' I admitted.

'Gled's an old Scots word for buzzard.'

Keith was looking into the wood. 'I see a feeder but no release pen,' he said.

'We only have one release pen,' Deeley said, 'and that's for the ex-laying birds. They went out weeks ago and with a bit of luck they're laying again in the wild. Our chicks are hatched and reared under broody hens. When we put them out, the hen keeps the chicks together and in place.'

'Old-fashioned but effective,' Keith said approvingly.

'Well, you wouldn't have turned any out here,' Penny said. 'They'd go plop into that barley and scatter and lose contact with the hen.'

'That's right,' Deeley said. 'The nearest are two hundred yards away, in bushes with grass all around. By the time they spread here, they'll be more worldly wise.'

Keith was nodding like an animated toy. 'I'll tell you something else,' he said. 'If Jim Broxburn was irresponsible enough to put out poisoned bait – which he wouldn't have been,' Keith added as Mr Deeley opened his mouth to protest, ' – nobody but a maniac would have done it here and this way. In a release pen, where no mammal could get at it, possibly. In a tunnel, just conceivably. But in the open like this and not attached to anything,

31

a bird of prey could have carried it off and dropped it where somebody's pet, or even his own dog, might find and eat it. And he didn't have any string in his pockets – right, Ralph?'

'Not according to the Sergeant,' I said. 'Is that why you wanted to know what he had in his pockets?'

'Obviously. If he'd had string, binder twine, something like that in his pocket, knowing nothing about his character I might have been able to believe the worst.'

I found another seat, on a boulder beside which the dogs were patiently waiting, while Penny and Keith walked small circles in the weeds and muttered incomprehensibly to each other and to Mr Deeley. The spaniel nosed my hand and I patted it, glad to know that somebody else was as baffled as I was.

'If there was ever anything interesting here,' Keith said at last, 'the police have lifted it. And if the procurator fiscal accepts that the death was accidental, they may discard anything that doesn't relate to the setting of poison. Ralph – ?'

'I'll make sure that nothing gets thrown away until we've seen it.'

'There's an old tunnel but no trap. I wonder what brought him here.'

They drifted back to me. Penny found a seat beside me. 'The police will have taken photographs,' she said. 'Could we get a look at them?'

'I can try,' I said. 'Sometimes they're co-operative, sometimes not. We may not see them unless or until they turn up in evidence.'

Something russet and streamlined swept over our heads and dropped suddenly towards the field. There was a shrill scream. 'What in hell was that?' I demanded.

'Male sparrowhawk,' Deeley said. 'The female has a nest back there. He'll be feeding her.'

'What did he catch? A rabbit?'

'Sparrowhawks usually only take birds,' he said. 'He's taking blackbirds and starlings now, but if the supply runs out when they have a growing brood to feed they may well turn to pheasant poults. And teach the young to do the same.'

The bird took off again and made a wide circle round us back to the wood, carrying what seemed to be a torn scrap of meat.

One of Keith's many annoying characteristics is a determination to solve every unrelated problem along the way instead of sticking to the main investigation. 'If I were you,' he said, 'I'd try to keep a supply of dead starlings. Put them down, one at a time, exactly where he made that kill, or at his plucking post if you can find it, with the breast plucked. And . . . But perhaps unasked advice irritates you?'

'Not a bit,' Deeley said with feeling. 'With Jim Broxburn not around, I need all the advice I can get.'

'Do you have a rubber or plastic decoy crow?' Keith asked him. 'Or an owl?'

'I think there's one of each among Jim Broxburn's pigeon decoys in the wash-house.'

'Mount one on a branch,' Keith said, 'on the side away from where you've put out your poults. Move it every day. Switch them around. When the female starts leaving the nest, as long as she takes it for a real predator it'll be against her instincts to leave in the other direction in case her nest gets robbed. If she stops believing it, try a magpie. I think the shop's got one in stock.'

'I'll try that,' Deeley said glumly. 'But it'll probably be stolen. Look what's coming across the field.'

'Mrs Spare-the-Sparrows Chegwin,' Keith said.

'All bosom and bluster,' Deeley confirmed. 'You can't leave a trap or a decoy where she can find it or it gets stolen. As far as she's concerned, even the Fenn trap's illegal. She thinks it's the same as a gin-trap.'

The lady advancing across the grass did indeed have a figure which had got out of hand; not with an enjoyable plumpness like Penny's but in a busty, tightly corseted way which reminded me of a pudding in a cloth. Her face was also reminiscent of the worse sort of pudding, being round, with a slight double chin and a short upper lip which would have given her mouth an angry expression even in repose. She wore an old macintosh despite the heat and a shapeless felt hat was perched over her hair. On her massive mammaries bounced a camera which even I could recognise as expensive.

'Is that her RSPB hat she's wearing?' Keith asked.

'Unfortunately not,' Deeley said. 'They're not allowed by their constitution to be anti-sporting, but by their nature they attract the fanatical protectionists.'

Penny saw that I was baffled again. 'Royal Society for the Protection of Birds,' she whispered. 'And a protectionist doesn't accept any need for species control.'

Mrs Chegwin opened her assault while she was still a good stone's throw away, but her piercing voice could have been heard in Newton Lauder. 'I suppose you're lying in wait for that unfortunate bird,' she cried.

Even I could see the silliness of the statement in view of the fact that none of us had as much as a pea-shooter to hand. But Deeley kept his temper admirably. 'As long as he limits himself to killing starlings,' he said, 'he'll be a welcome guest.' He put, I thought, a slight emphasis on the word 'killing' and again on the word 'he'.

Mrs Chegwin came to a halt, peering through the hedge like some creature of the wild. She managed to put a world of disbelief into a single sniff and a curl of the upper lip. 'If your Mr Broxburn wasn't laying bait for the sparrowhawk, he was laying it for my cat,' she stated.

Deeley looked at her as though he had caught her pouncing on one of his pheasants. 'If – and I don't admit it for one moment – but if Jim was laying bait at all it would certainly have been for your cat. And he would have had my support. I'd sooner have a fox around here than that blasted cat. Next time I see it near a partridge nest, I'll shoot it.'

'And have a lawsuit on your hands.' But Mrs Chegwin may have felt vulnerable on the subject of her cat's behaviour. She changed ground. 'He was certainly laying bait. And I can prove it.' She patted her camera. 'I'd come out early to photograph the sparrowhawk. I was going to hide in the edge of the wood and watch his favourite hunting territory and I found Mr Broxburn lying right in the middle of it with the syringe in his hand and the bottle nearby.'

'Did he have his gun with him?' Keith asked.

She shuddered. 'The horrid thing was lying a few yards away, leaning up against that stump.'

'If he knew where the nest was and he had his gun,' Keith said, 'he'd hardly go to the trouble of laying bait.'

'He was being sneaky,' Mrs Chegwin said hotly. 'I could have photographed him shooting a protected species; but it's much more difficult to prove a case of poisoning.'

'Was there any kind of small box or case nearby?' Keith asked.

'Not that I noticed.' She fired a suspicious look at him. 'Why?'

'I'm wondering how he would have carried a syringe and needle. You wouldn't drop a loaded syringe loose into a pocket. One careless movement – '

'I don't know and I don't care and, what's more, I don't have to answer any more questions,' Mrs Chegwin said. 'Sergeant Fuller said so. I've phoned the Health and

Safety Executive and they'll have some questions of their own to ask. Good day to you.'

She turned on her heel and stumped off.

'And a very good day to you too,' Deeley said. He lowered his voice. 'What was that about the Health and Safety Executive?' he asked me.

'If a court decided that Mr Broxburn was an employee,' I said, 'then, under the Health and Safety at Work Act, you or the syndicate could be vulnerable – for setting him to carry out an illegal task. And the onus would be on you to prove that he had been instructed in how to carry out the task safely, which you couldn't do without admitting the first offence.' As I spoke, it occurred to me that Jim Broxburn's estate might have a case against the syndicate, in which eventuality a sheriff might not approve of Mr Deeley's solicitor taking a hand in its administration for fear of a conflict of interests. For the moment, however, a degree of responsibility for the late Mr Broxburn's effects gave me a useful lever with the police. I decided to let matters ride for a little longer.

'It gets worse and worse, doesn't it?' Deeley said. 'Let's go back to the house.'

While we were speaking, Keith's spaniel had ambled over to near where the body had lain. It turned suddenly and came back to Keith's heel, shivering unhappily.

Deeley bent down to pat the dog. 'Amazing how they can smell death, isn't it?' he said.

'And other things,' Keith said slowly. 'Fear and hate among them. There've been many attempts to estimate how many times more powerful than a man's is a dog's sense of smell. Figures I've heard range between a thousand and a million.'

'That's a lot,' Deeley said. 'A pity he can't tell us what he knows.'

The hump in the centre of the track made it impossible

to walk more than two abreast, one in each wheel-rut. Keith and Alexander Deeley went ahead and Penny and I fell in behind. As we walked – or in my case, according to Penny, dawdled – back toward the house, Deeley began to speak. It was as though he was speaking compulsively in an effort to exclude the present.

'I've always loved this place,' he said. 'It belonged to an uncle of mine. An aunt's husband, to be more precise. I used to come here during the school holidays. We lived in Edinburgh but city life never suited me. The old chap used to let me use an old four-ten and my cousin and I kept down the pigeon and crows and rabbits for him.

'Later, while I was abroad, the old boy passed on. My cousin wrote to me. He preferred urban life and he had a growing career in engineering. Remembering my love of the place, he asked whether I'd like to buy it at valuation. I jumped at the chance. It took all my capital and there wasn't much of a return after I'd paid a succession of managers to look after it for me, but at least I had something to look forward to while I was sweating it out in some rather torrid jungles. I was in timber, you know, buying exotic woods for the top end of the furniture trade.' (I caught Penny's eye. It is not often that her grapevine is caught out in an inaccuracy.)

Deeley paused in mid-stride and leaned on Keith's shoulder while he kicked his heel to dislodge a small stone from his sandal and we closed the gap which had been widening between the striders up ahead and my more gentlemanly stroll, to which Penny had adjusted her own pace. 'Should have put proper boots on,' he said. 'I suppose the farm ought to have shown a good profit, the way farming was then; but I wanted the place as I remembered it and I wouldn't have them grub up a hedge or fell a tree.

'If I had a clear picture in my mind of what I wanted

37

to do with it, I suppose it was one of pottering quietly through my old age, helping around the farm and having a stroll with the gun, reliving my boyhood. I tried it for a while and was bored out of my mind. I suppose I'd moved on. The small boy who'd been as happy as a lark stalking rabbits or waiting for pigeon to come into a wood was gone for ever.

'Then I found that a neighbouring farmer was interested in the idea of a syndicate and that the sporting rights to the two other farms were up for lease. So we formed the syndicate. It's not very high up the market. The first requirement for membership isn't money, it's being a safe gun and the sort of man who's a pleasure to spend the day with and who's prepared to turn out and help whoever's doing the keepering. If he has a wife and daughters who can join the beating line, so much the better.' He sighed and slashed at an inoffensive weed with his stick. His voice was becoming fainter as he and Keith drew ahead again. 'I've enjoyed the last few years. Not just the shooting but the whole scene. You might call it gardening for birds. I only hope that we can salvage something out of this disaster.'

'It isn't a disaster until it happens,' Keith said. 'Except from the viewpoint of the dead man, of course.'

The track forked. Mr Deeley led us round the back of the house. Beyond a small paddock marked with neat rectangles of scraped and yellowed grass, two adjoining cottages faced the house. From the door of one, a woman looked at us stonily before retreating indoors.

Deeley led us to a door in an outbuilding. 'This is the keeper's store,' he said, unlocking it. 'Broxburn and I held the only keys.'

'How easy is that rat-poison to obtain?' I asked him.

'It's commonplace around farms. I don't know whether the public can buy it.'

It was a cool room even on that hot day; whitewashed and much of it lined with rough shelving neatly stacked with gear. I was able to recognise pigeon and duck decoys, camouflage nets, wire snares and some metal contraptions which Penny confirmed were traps. Against the walls were stacked sections of some construction in wire netting and corrugated iron, leaving a reduced floorspace on which we were crowded together. An Ordnance Survey map, heavily annotated in pencil, was pinned to the large sheet of fibreboard which took up part of one wall.

Keith gravitated to the map. 'The circles mark where the broody hens were turned out?'

'That's right,' Deeley said.

'So the crosses mark his traps?'

'Right again. He does . . . did a different line each week. The traps aren't ideally sited, but if they were put where Mrs Chegwin could find them, she stole them. What a pity that we've no law of trespass in Scotland!'

Deeley paused. He removed his panama hat to reveal a thinning head of silvery hair through which he ran his fingers. He was looking harassed. 'I only hope that Jim kept the plan up to date. I don't suppose he finished his round this morning. I'll have to visit them this afternoon. Sir Peter promised to lend me the occasional services of a forester who helps his own keeper out in times of stress. He can do the heavy work, humping feed and water to the feeding points, but he won't have time to visit the traps every day as the law requires. The syndicate members are turning out for a working party at the weekend, but one day's help visiting traps would be more trouble than it's worth.'

'You'll be busy today,' Keith said. 'I'll go round them this afternoon, if you like. Can I borrow this map? And do you mind if I fold it?'

'If you're sure,' Deeley said. 'I would certainly appreciate the help. I've a photocopy of the plan you could copy the positions of the traps on to.' We heard the beat of a heavy engine outside. 'Now what?' he said. 'Can't be the Health and Safety people already, surely. Not more police?' He took a look through the dusty window. 'No, it's McAngel, the falconer I mentioned. I'll see what he wants. Excuse me.'

He went out and a few seconds later I heard his voice from near the window. I was curious enough to take a look. The man emerging from a dusty Land-rover was overpowering in size – tall, heavily built and running to fat. He had a bushy, reddish beard.

His voice, in contrast, was piping. It was as though a bull had cheeped like a sparrow. 'I heard about the accident to Jimmy Broxburn,' he was saying. 'Very sad. I called round to ask if there wasn't anything I could do.'

'Very good of you,' Deeley said in a loud voice. 'No, I don't think there's anything you could do. What did you have in mind?'

'You'll be stuck for a keeper. I could help out.'

'From what I hear, you're too busy even to spend much time with your falcons. Were you thinking of taking over Jim's half-gun?'

McAngel laughed shrilly. 'Nothing like that,' he said. 'You'd have your half-gun in hand. I'd be satisfied with permission to fly my falcons over the syndicate's land now and again.'

Deeley's voice, which had been loud, rose higher. 'Over . . . my . . . dead . . . body!' he said.

'I don't see why,' McAngel persisted. 'Don't you think that you're being a wee bit unreasonable? I wouldn't expect to take a quarter of the birds Jim Broxburn shot in a season.'

Through the dusty glass I clearly heard Mr Deeley's

40

snort of mirthless laughter. 'After our birds had been stooped at and missed a few times, they'd never fly high. They'd prefer hedge-hopping. And at least Jim Broxburn could tell the difference between a full-grown pheasant and an immature cheeper.'

'I see that there's no reasoning with you,' McAngel said sadly. 'Well, let me know if you change your mind.'

'Don't hold your breath,' Deeley said firmly.

THREE

The morning had, if not flown, at least stumbled its way
into the past. When it appeared that we were staying to
lunch, I made no protest. We were already too late for
lunch at Whisbeck Grange.

Mrs Deeley, when we met her, was a small, housewifely
woman. Small women tend to become dumpy in later life
but she had kept her figure well into middle age, although
she had made no attempt to camouflage the grey tints in
her sandy hair. She was shocked by Broxburn's death, as
she would have been shocked by the death of anyone
within her small acquaintance, but although we discussed
the circumstances over a cold lunch she seemed to be deaf
to any implications beyond the death itself.

A layer of cloud had crept down from the north, obscu-
ring the sun and somehow echoing Alexander Deeley's
mood. The heat had gone out of the day, for which I
was thankful. We ate in a dining room which seemed
dark after the morning's brightness. I was glad to rest
my bones.

'Was Jim Broxburn left-handed?' Keith asked suddenly. 'The writing on the map had a back-handed
slant.'

'I never noticed,' Deeley admitted. 'He certainly shot
off his left shoulder, but that could have been because of
faulty vision in his right eye.'

'He was left-handed,' Mrs Deeley said. 'I noticed. He brought me in a pigeon sometimes, or a rabbit for Ringo's dinner, and he was always very good about plucking or skinning them for me. Why did you want to know?'

Instead of answering, Keith addressed Mr Deeley. 'Do you have a pen on you?'

Deeley took a fountain pen out of his pocket and held it out.

'Keep it,' Keith said. 'Imagine that it's a syringe and that your bread roll is a dead pheasant chick. Pretend to inject it.' He waited while Deeley fumbled with the two objects. 'Now, your hand slips. Which hand do you jab yourself in?'

'The left,' Deeley said.

'Like Jim Broxburn. But if you'd been left-handed?'

His questions were clearly rhetorical. 'I see what you're getting at,' I said. 'But people sometimes do things cack-handed. It could well be argued that that's how he came to be clumsy enough to inject himself. You'll need more substantial evidence than that if we're going to convince a sheriff that he didn't die from a simple accident while poisoning bait for hawks.'

'But of course it was a simple accident,' Mrs Deeley said.

'It may have been, but you can't possibly know,' her husband said irritably. 'You were in bed. You sleep most of the morning.'

'It's the only time I can get any real sleep,' she said. 'You toss and turn for half the night and then get up at the crack of dawn.'

'I don't need as much sleep as I used to,' Deeley said more pacifically. 'By the time I hear Jim Broxburn's old van, I'm usually awake. I suppose I shan't be hearing that any more.' He paused and gave a small shiver. 'Somehow that makes it more real. Until now, I've been thinking of his death as an incident. It's only now coming home to me that from now on . . . nothing will ever be quite the same again.'

'Did you hear the van this morning?' Keith asked.

'Yes. He'd been at work overnight. Jim used to arrive back from the bakery at any time after five,' he explained, 'and he'd stop at our door to drop Rabbie off. Then I'd go down to let Ringo out. The two are bosom buddies and they'd stay by the front door until he came back. I suppose Rabbie will be a permanency around here now,' he said thoughtfully. 'If Jim ever made a will, I don't suppose he specified the dog; and I don't see the sister wanting Rabbie sent out to Canada. Well, he's a good old boy and I dare say we can give him a good home and some work to do.

'Jim always liked to go round his traps first thing. He said that the walk in the fresh air helped him to sleep, and it gave time for Ron Aicheson to start up the tractor and get out of earshot. The rest of the keepering work could usually wait until after he'd slept.'

'He brought in a pigeon that had been killed by a hawk a few days ago,' Mrs Deeley said. 'You could still see the marks of the talons. Jim said that a second pigeon came over and the hawk took up the chase again. Jim came to me for a recipe. He was calling the sparrowhawks all the names he could think of, because one had taken a pheasant chick and he said that when they'd found one easy meal they'd always go back for more. I said why didn't he do something about them and he said that he probably would. There's cheese and biscuits,' she added, 'and I'll bring coffee in a minute.'

'I hope to God you didn't tell that to the police,' Deeley said.

'Well, you never tell me anything,' Mrs Deeley said

defensively, 'so I asked one of the young policemen what was going on and he told me what seemed to have happened and I told him what Jim had said to me.'

Deeley's eyes were beginning to pop. I prepared to feign deafness to a flaming marital row but Penny spoke quickly before flashpoint could be reached. 'What exactly did Jim Broxburn say?'

'I've just *told* you – '

'His exact words. Did he say "I'll do it"? Or "I may do it"? Or "I'll think about it"? Please think back, Mrs Deeley. It could be important.'

'All right, my dear. Give me a moment.' She got up to fetch coffee. When she was seated again, she said, 'He used one of those expressions with the word "mind" in it. "I've a good mind" or "I've half a mind". You know what I mean. Does it matter?'

'But which?' Penny asked. 'Please. It could matter a lot.'

'I don't see why but I'll try. Yes, I remember,' she said triumphantly. 'He said "I've half a mind". I noticed, because if ever there was anybody who had more than half a mind it was Jim Broxburn. He was always so positive about things.'

I breathed a sigh of relief and I think that Alexander Deeley did the same. 'I've half a mind' is an expression which people use of something which they have no intention of doing. 'If the police speak to you again,' I said, 'please try to give them those exact words.' It was a minor point in the face of all the other evidence, but sometimes the only defence is to attack the other side's points one by one.

'What did you do after you were up?' Keith asked Mr Deeley. 'I suppose you didn't see or hear anything?'

'I had a quick breakfast. I never take more than a bowl of cereal. Then I went to have a word with Ron.

Sometimes he can use an extra pair of hands. But this is the quiet time of the year, waiting for crops to ripen. When the rape's ready to harvest he'll be glad enough of some help. And we'll be cutting silage soon.'

'And then you woke me up again, mowing the grass,' his wife said.

'I did cut the grass. I have one of those sit-on machines and I wouldn't see or hear anything while I was sitting on it. After that, I made a cup of tea and took one up to Betty.'

'Waking me up once more,' Mrs Deeley said. She shot her husband a look which was half teasing and half malicious. 'There'll be a vacancy in the night-shift at the bakery,' she said. 'Why don't you apply for it and let me get some sleep? It isn't as if we couldn't do with the money.'

We left the lunch table – thanking our hostess politely, because even a cold lunch with soggy lettuce demands a certain degree of courtesy. She had meant well.

Penny's first husband had been a farmer who ended his life under an overturned tractor and although her few references to him had been less than flattering I believe that she still hankered for the rural life. She elected to accompany Keith, who promised to return her to Newton Lauder when they had finished the round of the traps, while I made a preliminary inspection of Jim Broxburn's chattels. His cottage, Deeley told me, was never locked.

I walked across the paddock from one gate to the other, following a well-trodden path. The rectangular markings, Deeley had said, were where the brooder coops had stood. A battered but serviceable van stood on a patch of worn earth. I pushed open the cottage door and went inside.

From next door, I could hear the sound of a radio or television and a woman's voice scolding a child, but in Broxburn's cottage all was quiet. A dwelling seems to know when its occupant has died. I tried to sense an atmosphere but instead I found that I was drawing conclusions.

Starting from the pair of slippers placed neatly together just inside the door, the place was tidy. If the police had looked inside they had not deemed it necessary to make a search. The cleanliness would have put many a housewife to shame. The almost imperceptible dust had not lain there for more than a day. And, very unusually for a bachelor dwelling, it even smelled clean – not the deodorised and perfumed smell of a woman's house; just clean.

Deeley had suggested that the dead man had had ideals but it struck me, for reasons that I could not have put into words, that this was not the finicky tidiness of the perfectionist but the orderliness of a busy and methodical man. Things were not pushed into exact alignment but were neatly in the place where they would be wanted next.

Everything was well worn, utilitarian yet suitable. Broxburn had not afforded expensive trivia but he had not needed them. The one soft chair in the sitting room was a clean but worn wing-chair. I settled in it while I studied the place and found it surprisingly comfortable. The seat had been altered to relieve any pressure on the user's coccyx. A small cushion had been attached just where it was needed to support the small of the back, while if I had been a few inches taller a second cushion would have been perfect for a head support. Padding had been added to the arms so that a man's elbows would be supported while he was reading. It had been modified, simply and without effort, into the ideal chair for a tired man. No woman would have tolerated it in the house but the makers, I thought, would have done well to study it. A comfortable chair is as rare and precious as a comfortable woman.

At my elbow, a makeshift shelf supported a row of books, mainly on keepering and wildlife. A tube of glue and a pair of scissors in front of the books led my eye to a fat scrapbook and I took it down. Mostly, it was filled with snippets from sporting magazines giving advice about keepering and dog training, but there were some newspaper cuttings about cases of poaching and of cruelty to animals, and one of the last entries referred to an illegal traffic in birds of prey.

Broxburn's office was represented by a smaller room containing a hard chair and a trestle table. The walls had been papered with pictures from girly calendars but his taste ran to pretty eroticism rather than downright pornography. His filing system was a row of cardboard cartons and large, brown envelopes. His papers would have to be removed and studied, but that would be the job of an executor. Each envelope was marked with the subject of its contents. Most of them had to do with the syndicate and its keepering. Under 'Business Personal', there was no sign of a will but I found a building-society deposit book. I was putting it away when I jerked it out and took another look at the balance. Over £11,000 seemed a remarkable balance for a bakery worker and part-time gamekeeper. The account had been opened with a single deposit two years earlier. No further deposits had been made and the withdrawals had been few and modest. The single deposit made it unlikely that this was the accumulation of years of thrift, unless he had transferred the account from elsewhere; but, of course, he might have received a legacy.

I put the envelope back in its place. Another envelope

marked 'Correspondence Personal' gave me the address of the sister in Canada.

The kitchen was large, clean and uninspired but, to judge from the contents of the larder, Broxburn had eschewed the convenience foods usually favoured by bachelors and had treated himself to proper meals, making full use of the produce of the farm and the countryside.

Broxburn's bedroom told me nothing. It contained a bed and a cheap wardrobe holding serviceable clothes and one good but inexpensive suit. It was a room for sleeping and dressing in and nothing more. There was a tiny spare bedroom which showed little sign of ever having been used and a severe, uncomfortable bathroom.

I found another room tucked into the back of the cottage. Broxburn had evidently used it as his personal workshop and store. A narrow steel cupboard stood open which would have held his shotgun. He seemed to have had only the one gun, and that was twelve-bore – I could read as much on the boxes of cartridges. Some of the tools on the bench I recognised as being for gun cleaning. A fishing rod lay across hooks in the wall. All the odds and ends, from screws to fishing line, had been collected in plastic boxes and neatly labelled. I looked into the only unlabelled box. A few white feathers – for fly-tying, I supposed.

There seemed to be nothing more that I could, or should, do for the moment. I had never met Jim Broxburn but I decided that I would have liked him. I locked the front door with the huge key which was in the lock – no wonder, I thought, that the place had usually stood open if the alternative was to carry this monster around.

As I fumbled with the heavy key, a man in dungarees emerged from the other cottage. I had the impression that he had been waiting inside the door so that he could meet me by apparent chance. He had a nervous, intelligent look. A cleft chin gave emphasis to a discontented mouth. His dark, collar-length hair looked slightly greasy.

'Hello,' he said with an attempt at a smile. 'You're the legal eagle, aren't you?' His accent was good and I decided that he must be one of the new breed of farmers with a diploma from an agricultural college in the pocket of his overalls.

'And you must be Mr Aicheson, the farm manager,' I replied.

He seemed undecided whether to shake hands. 'Terrible thing about Jim Broxburn,' he said at last.

I agreed and the conversation seemed about to die. He glanced nervously over his shoulder at the doorway where I guessed his wife was listening, out of sight.

'Look,' he said suddenly, 'I know it's early to talk about it, but if the subject comes up . . . It was never right that Jim should have the larger of the two cottages, a single man on his own. I've got a wife and two kids and we're living on top of each other. But Jim was already installed when I arrived. He wouldn't move and Mr Deeley wouldn't make him. Do you think Mr Deeley would let me move next door now?'

'I'm sure he'd consider it,' I said. 'As you say, it's early days. Of course, he'll probably want a cottage for another keeper and the best man may turn out to be somebody with two ladyfriends and a dozen children.'

That contingency had not occurred to him. He fell silent, but when I moved off towards the house he fell into step with me.

Sometimes I wish that I knew more about farming. I would have liked to say something wise about the soil or the weather or the crops but I had to fall back on asking him whether it was going to be a good year.

51

He snorted like an unsettled horse. 'It's never a good year,' he said. 'How could it be? He never lets me hire any regular help except for old Fergus, who can't get on with machinery and develops a bad back every pay-day.' The mention of Fergus put a fresh idea into his mind. 'Fergus lives in a caravan up at the back of the barn. If the next keeper's another single man, couldn't he take the caravan and let Fergus have my cottage and I'd take the bigger one?'

'You'd have to speak to Mr Deeley about that,' I said. 'Perhaps Fergus could share a cottage with the new keeper.'

He shook his head emphatically. 'Nobody would want to share a cottage with Fergus,' he said.

More to turn the subject than for any other reason, I asked him whether he had seen anybody that morning.

'Not in the way you mean,' he said. 'I'll tell you something though. There was a wind in the night and I heard Jim's door slam. I wondered if he'd been taken ill and come home, so I knocked on the wall and called out to ask whether he was all right. You can hear a fart through those walls,' he added parenthetically and then, as though to make up for a remark which had been out of keeping with the solemn circumstances, he went on, 'I liked Jim, I really did, so when I got no answer I was ready to go round and see how he was. But I heard somebody's feet running off. So I went round and fetched his key away and I put it back first thing this morning.'

'Nothing seemed to have been disturbed,' I said, 'so you probably scared somebody off before he could steal anything. Did Mr Broxburn have any valuables?'

'Not that I know of. I was hardly ever inside his door.'

'I think you should tell the police. What did you see this morning?'

'I was going to tell Jim that he'd had an intruder

and that he should be more careful about locking up, but I only saw him in the distance while I was fitting the spray bars on the tractor and filling up with insecticide. He was walking up past Gled Corner to visit his traps, but I was going to head the other way. Mr Deeley caught me before I left, to give me his usual lecture about leaving an unsprayed headland alongside every hedge. And how I'm supposed to show a profit while he's determined to farm for the shooting I'm damned if I know!'

'Surely that's his worry rather than yours,' I suggested.

We had come to a halt near the house. He lowered his voice. 'But how do I explain it, next time I go for a job interview? All they want to know about is profitability. But Mr Deeley, he just wants to play at being a farmer. Not doing any real work but driving around on the tractor, knocking down gates and spilling his load. You have to keep your eyes on what you're doing when you're driving a tractor, that's why I didn't see anybody. If there was anybody to see,' he added quickly.

I would have liked to escape before he infected me with his discontent, but there was one question to be asked. 'Do you think that Jim Broxburn would have laid poisoned bait for birds of prey?'

He considered the question seriously for a moment. 'Damned if I know,' he said at last. 'He had strong views about wildlife and the law. On the other hand, he thought that the sun shone out of his pheasants' tiny arseholes. He'd be torn between the two forces and God knows which way he'd end up going. Anyway, if the police say that that's what he was doing, then I'll believe it.' He shot a look at a digital wristwatch. 'I'll have to be going. If the tenancy of the cottage is mentioned, you won't forget?'

'I won't forget,' I said. But that was not to promise that I would do anything about it.

I found Mrs Deeley in her spacious kitchen and asked her whether she wished to lay claim to the food in Jim Broxburn's kitchen before it went bad. The disagreement with her husband seemed to be rankling and she said rather huffily that she could manage without second-hand food. So I went back to the cottages and bestowed the perishables on Ron Aicheson's wife, a surly woman with a squint, who refused to utter a word of pleasure or thanks although I could tell that she was pleased.

I left the key of the keeper's cottage with Mr Deeley and drove carefully back to Newton Lauder.

FOUR

My office was still quiet, although Miss Jelks had managed to work up a head of steam over some quite trivial correspondence. I dictated a letter or two and then took up the phone.

Canada would be up and doing by now. Overseas Directory Enquiries found me a phone number for Jim Broxburn's brother-in-law, Ferguson by name and resident near Montreal. In a short time I was connected, via a surprisingly clear line, to a female voice with an agreeable mixture of Scots and Canadian accents.

One unpleasant duty was spared me. Notification of her brother's death had already reached her through the police, who had no doubt followed up the letter in the dead man's pocket.

Quickly, because I was bearing the cost of a transatlantic call without any certainty of reimbursement, I introduced myself and explained my somewhat peripheral concern in the matter. She grasped the salient points immediately. 'As far as I know,' she said, 'my brother never made a will.'

'The proper course would be to petition the Sheriff Court to appoint you his executor,' I explained.

'But I'm a long way off and I wouldn't know how to go about being an executor, especially at such long range.'

'You could then appoint a local solicitor to act on your behalf. I'm not touting for work,' I added hastily. 'I can suggest other names if you wish.'

'It all seems a bit of a kerfuffle,' she said unhappily.

'It's necessary,' I said. 'In view of the size of the estate . . .'

'What estate? Jim was never up there among the Carnegies.'

I was reluctant to mention figures, not least because these might imply that her brother had been Up To Something. 'He had quite a sum deposited with a building society,' I said.

'Oh yes,' she said immediately. 'I was forgetting. He and a few of his friends at the bakery had a pools win, a year or two ago. I thought he'd have blown it by now. That's what I told him to do. How much is left of it?'

I breathed a sigh of relief. The money was explained. 'About eleven thousand,' I said. 'Pounds.'

'Really? I didn't know that his share was as much as that to start off with. Look,' she said, 'I'll be coming over for the funeral.'

'We can't be sure when that will be,' I said. 'They're certain to hold a Fatal Accident Enquiry. Your brother's body should be released after the pathologist has finished his examination, but it all takes time.'

'I'll come over anyway. This has caught me by surprise, but . . . Go ahead and petition the sheriff or whatever you said. Shall I send you a cable to confirm?'

'Please,' I said. 'Do you want me to make any funeral arrangements in readiness for when the body's released?'

She was businesslike and unsentimental about it. 'Jim never wanted to clutter up the ground in some cemetery that he'd never seen before. He wanted to be cremated. And Ladyhill Woods was the only place he'd been happy.

He wanted his ashes scattered there. That wouldn't take long to fix?'

'Not long at all,' I said.

Miss Jelks had, as usual, been listening on the other phone. She had been preparing to go home but she offered to stay late. I sent her packing. Little though I liked mechanical contrivances there was one area of modern technology which I considered a godsend. I much preferred dictating into a recorder than to somebody who would sigh and look put upon whenever I made a correction. I hunted out a copy of a similar petition and dictated a revised version on to tape, to be typed up in the morning.

I locked up and walked the few yards to the hotel. I had stiffened with sitting and my hips and ankles were protesting that they had borne my weight enough for one day. The bars were busy and Penny had already had her break, so I dined alone in a corner of the lounge bar, on microwaved scampi and chips with a glass or two of too dry a wine. It had been an interesting day but gastronomically a disaster.

There was nobody among the crowd in the bar whom I both knew and cared to chat with, so I went home to our flat in the upper floor of what had once been a large Victorian house and dozed for a while over a glass of brandy in front of the television. The material on TV is usually no worse than the films which I was accustomed to attend, despite considerable expense and hideously uncomfortable seats, in my youth; indeed, very often the same films comprise the only programmes worth watching. That evening, however, I had seen both films years earlier and disliked them both, while the sitcoms were transparent and contrived. I watched the news before deciding to head for bed.

I heard Penny come in while I was under the shower,

but several minutes later I found her brushing her hair before the bedroom mirror, showing no signs of having started to undress.

'You poor old thing!' she said into the mirror. 'Did we walk you too far?' With woman's logic, she was inclined to be brisk and unsympathetic by day and to relent after nightfall.

I was feeling a little more supple after my shower. 'Did it show?' I asked.

'You were hobbling rather when you left the hotel.'

'Once around you is getting to be too far,' I admitted.

She either failed or refused to see the ungallant implication. 'I'll try to remember that you're not a boy any more. Lie down on your tum and I'll give you a massage. But you do lay it on a bit thick sometimes.'

'I do not,' I protested. 'As a matter of fact, I put a very brave face on it.'

She chuckled indulgently and came over to the bed.

Being massaged by Penny did little for joints which had lost their resilience but it was an enjoyable experience. I lay face down on the bed and felt her thumbs seeking out the knots of fibrositis.

'I'm trying to be specially nice to you,' she explained, 'just to make up.'

'It's all right,' I said. 'I prefer you to remember me as I was, young and athletic.'

'You were never that. Not while I knew you. What happened after we left you?'

Penny is a listener rather than a talker or I would never have married her. I knew that confidences would be safe between her ears. Despite the muffling effect of the pillow I managed to tell her about my afternoon. When I mentioned Ron Aicheson, the farm manager, I felt her fingers give a little jab of impatience. 'He's a gype, than man,' she said. 'He got well on in the public bar one night and he was greeting about how hard done by he is. He doesn't know when he's well off. With farming having to diversify these days, there's plenty of estates glad to employ a farmer who knows about shooting. He should be taking a pride in it and trying to learn.' She gave me a gentle smack on my bottom. 'Turn over.'

I turned over. She got to work on my thigh and stomach muscles. I relaxed luxuriously. Her touch was reminding me of earlier days, when fleshly contact had been charged with electricity and magic. 'It's human nature to grumble,' I said.

'Maybe. But he can't have it both ways. If he's going for job interviews, why is he so desperate to swap cottages?'

'Hedging his bets,' I said. 'What did you and Keith discover?'

'We found all the traps. Three rats and a weasel. I don't think we led Mrs Chegwin to any of them. And we had a good look around. But you know Keith – anything he says while he's thinking is too obscure to make head or tail of. He picked up whatever seemed even remotely interesting, from old shotgun cartridges to a lens out of somebody's sunglasses, some binder twine and a brass case from a two-two rifle – or it might have been one of those blanks that dog trainers use with a dummy launcher. That was about a quarter of a mile up the hill from the house, not far from one of the traps. The grass seemed to me to have been flattened over an area about the size of this bed, but Keith only grunted. I didn't see any feathers there.'

Penny crawled on to the bed and knelt astride me. She spread her pleated skirt so that it covered me from the knees to the lower chest and went to work on my pectoral muscles. The movement of her hands was transmitted through her body. 'When we got back to the house, Mr

59

Deeley asked Keith how much he'd charge for going on and finding out exactly what had happened. Keith said that he wasn't a private eye – he always says that, doesn't he? – but I could tell that he was bursting with curiosity. In the end, he said that he'd do it in exchange for Jim Broxburn's half-gun next season.'

'Wallace will love that!' I said absently. Wallace James, Keith's partner, strongly disapproved of any activity which distracted Keith from strict attention to business unless a substantial fee was brought back in return.

'Wallace won't mind. In the car, Keith said that he was going to share the half-gun with him, turn about. And Wal's just as crazy as Keith, really.'

Between times, I had begun to see myself as looking down from an Olympian height on a human race driven by the demands of their bodies. But now, under the spread skirt, strange half-forgotten wonders were happening. I had been mistaken on one point. Penny had certainly begun to undress.

On the following morning I had to go into Edinburgh. The long drive was made bearable by a screen of cloud which kept the heat out of the day.

One of Newton Lauder's more enterprising sons had asked for my services. He had much earlier visited the bank manager, showing him a letter accepting his offer for an expensive house with an occupation date still two months off and another letter from the manager of the building society explaining that withdrawal of the substantial sum on three-month deposit before the expiry of the period of notice would cost him his interest over the whole three-month period. Obviously it would be sounder economics to bridge the gap by borrowing the same sum from the bank for the few weeks between the purchase date and the end of the period of notice. The bank manager, delighted to make such a closed-ended loan, had agreed.

Unfortunately, my new client had produced the same documents and reached the same agreement with eight other banks between Newton Lauder and Edinburgh, intending, it was supposed, to disappear with all the money plus his original capital. However, he had made the mistake of approaching more than one branch of the same bank, and his arrest had followed.

My client was a plain and very ordinary man who had for once been overtaken by a sudden and unjustified belief in his own guile. It took most of the morning to vet his story, accompany him before the sheriff and then assure him that, the police having made their own mistake of pouncing before more than two such loans had been made, we had at least a sporting change of inducing a jury to believe that his approaches to the banks had been for purposes of comparison only and that after obtaining the first loan he had changed his mind and claimed the second for the sake of a minuscule percentage of interest, intending to repay the first immediately. A judge would have taken the story with more than a pinch of salt, but juries can be remarkably credulous.

I was back in Newton Lauder by mid-afternoon and called on my client's wife to offer the same comfort – this although I strongly suspected, thanks to intelligence garnered by Penny over the bar, that he had intended to use the money to decamp with the bank manager's secretary, who had put him up to it in the first place. A lingering mood of post-coital calm helped me to get through an interview which was distinctly fractious. The lady, it seemed, had her own suspicions.

I dictated similar letters to the two banks pointing out that, thanks to their precipitate and unjustified action, their money was now frozen in my client's current account and that they need therefore expect no interest to be paid on it. The house purchase had fallen through and both loans would be repaid as soon as the silly misunderstanding was cleared up.

After that, I was free to return my attention to matters at Ladyhill Woods.

The cable had arrived from Jim Broxburn's sister, so I collected the typed petition from Miss Jelks and deposited it at the Sheriff Court before going on to my next port of call.

The bakery in Newton Lauder is small for the growing population it serves, so it works a two-shift system. Cakes and pies are produced by day. Then, overnight, different personnel who appreciate a better pay-scale, more flexible hours and the chance of a nap while the ovens do the real work turn out the next day's bread and rolls.

The day-shift was finishing up but I knew that Mr Spence, the night manager, whom I had once defended, unsuccessfully, on a drunk-driving charge, always arrived in good time to take over. I was in luck. He was not only in but he was free for the moment.

My failure to save him from the results of his own folly had been forgiven and forgotten. It took only a minute or two to settle the question of outstanding wages. Broxburn's contributions to the Savings Club took a little longer.

When we had finished our immediate business, Spence took me into his tiny office. He was a large man and running to fat. His round face was marred by a disproportionately small and neat moustache.

'I'll miss Jim,' he said. 'He could be a pain in the backside at times, but he was always clean and always willing. He took a sudden night off now and again – he did it to me on Monday – but on the other hand he never minded working overtime if I was in a spot. What exactly did happen?' While we spoke he was changing his shoes for carpet slippers. Since losing his driving licence he walked to work and his feet sometimes troubled him.

'That's what we all want to know,' I said. 'Superficially, the evidence suggests that he accidentally jabbed the poison into his own hand while laying poisoned bait for birds of prey.'

'That would be illegal, wouldn't it?'

'Very.'

'Then that's not what happened,' Spence said firmly. 'Jim's view was that if you didn't agree with the law you didn't break it, you fought to have it changed. He was always getting up petitions and he was a thorn in the flesh of the councillors. The local MP ran for cover whenever Jim showed his face. And I've heard him lecturing the lads on everything from TV licences to poll tax. His message was "Shut up grumbling and pay your whack".'

That seemed to accord with Mr Deeley's opinion. But it was not easy to envisage how else Broxburn could have died in those unusual circumstances. A sneeze at an unpropitious moment seemed more likely than any other explanation. Unless, of course, he had had an enemy . . .

'How did he get along with people?' I asked.

'So-so. He could rub them up the wrong way. But there were rarely any hard feelings as far as he was concerned.'

'And as far as they were concerned?'

He shrugged. 'Who knows? Some folk can seem to forget a bit of needle, but years later you find that it's still rankling. Is there nobody you hate who'd be amazed to know it?'

Thinking it over I realised that there were probably dozens, from a punk rocker who had once addressed me as Porky to the man who invented plastic packaging. 'Was there anybody in particular at daggers drawn with Jim Broxburn?' I asked.

'Not that I know of,' Spence said thoughtfully. 'Unless somebody's husband found out and lost the heid.'

'You surprise me,' I said. 'Everybody's been telling me that he was a man of conscience.'

'And so he was, about every other thing. He never said much about it, mind you, but I got the impression that he stayed single because he was comfortably established with a married lady. His workmates knew something, because there was always a nudge and a wink when Jim took one of his sudden nights off.

'Also, there was somebody Jim was getting his knife into but I don't know who it was. About a fortnight back, he was raging about somebody who he said was making a fortune outside the law but he couldn't prove it. Yet, he said. He couldn't prove it yet. He didn't say what it was about. Deer poaching would be my guess. He always hated deer poachers. Do you think that he was murdered?'

'Good God no!' I said. The possibility had crossed my mind, but as a potential red rag for the constabulary bull rather than as a viable theory. 'Did he ever consult a solicitor?'

'He was going to,' Spence said. 'Two nights before he died, he asked for the name of a good lawyer. I gave him yours. He never said what it was about.'

We took a look in Jim Broxburn's locker. Spence said that the few odds and ends could remain there meantime. In the pocket of his white overall I found a slip of paper on which the words 'Saturday night!!!' had been written in a decisive hand. I looked at it for some seconds before deciding that, while the hand could have been either male or female, it certainly did not have Jim Broxburn's backhanded slant.

FIVE

On the next day, the Friday, I was due in the Sheriff Court to defend a client. He was accused of causing a road accident in the hope of replacing his old car at the expense of the other party.

After a day's respite, the sun had emerged again, although with a less savage heat than before. While the sheriff dealt with some minor business in chambers, I took to a bench on the grass outside and relaxed in the warmth of a perfect day. I closed my eyes against the brightness. My mental sifting of the facts and arguments in the case to come was beginning to melt into the illogicality of a dream when a voice suddenly spoke my name.

I snapped awake. A woman was standing, looking down at me. She looked tired but amused. 'I'm Ann Ferguson,' she said.

Considering my abrupt awakening from a light doze, it was a feat to recognise the name immediately and to connect it with Jim Broxburn's sister. The mixture of Scottish and transatlantic accents helped. I invited her to join me on the bench.

She thanked me and sat down, neatly. Her face and figure were ordinary, but her brown hair had been well dressed and her clothes, although not quite in line with current British fashion, were good. Her legs, in the previous year's shorter skirt, were even better. 'I flew in at some terrible hour this morning,' she said. 'So I hired a car at Edinburgh and drove straight out. I was told that I'd find you here.'

I tried to find the correct, sympathetic words. She accepted them and then put them aside.

'I'm not going to weep for my brother,' she said. 'He wouldn't have expected it. You know, a neighbour of ours has a disc on which one of your actors – John Le Mesurier – is reading a Red Indian poem. I remember how it begins. "When I am dead, cry for me a little. Think of me sometimes but not too much." That just about sums it up. I've had my cry and now I've come over to see to the business.'

'I hope that you haven't wasted your trip,' I said. 'A date for the Fatal Accident Enquiry hasn't been set yet and the procurator fiscal seems to be in no hurry to release your brother's body. I can try to chase up the petition to have you appointed as executor.' I saw my client waving at me from the steps. 'My case is being called,' I said. 'It may take a little time.'

'I'll go check into the hotel and come back,' she said.

'Perfect. If I'm not sitting here, look for me inside.'

I hurried into the courtroom and we went through the preliminaries for a trial. Then, when my client was invited to plead, he suddenly changed his plea to guilty. Because the flash of headlights by means of which he had advised the overtaking lorry that it would be safe to return to his lane had been seen by a dozen witnesses, I had been advising him for weeks to do exactly that; but by leaving his change of plea until the last moment, in the vain hope that each of the witnesses might be smitten with amnesia or struck by lightning, he had caused a great deal of wasted trouble and expense to the prosecution, the witnesses and, not least, to myself. If there was any plea to be made in mitigation, except to emphasise his previous good behaviour and to point out that he had already penalised himself to the tune of one motor car, I was not in the mood to think of it. I said what I could and it must have sufficed, because although the sheriff dealt with him severely, he was more lenient than I would have been.

The next case had been called for the afternoon. The sheriff rose. Looking round, I saw that Mrs Ferguson was among the spectators. I beckoned to her and whispered urgently to the clerk, who followed the sheriff out of the courtroom.

The sheriff allowed the room to empty before he returned and resumed his throne.

'You have a petition, Mr Enterkin?'

'M'lud.'

The sheriff, unlike some of his kind, was a sharp old man with a memory like a rat-trap. 'If this refers to the death of James Broxburn and the appointment of his sister as executor, I have already looked at your submission. Why has the matter suddenly become urgent?'

'Mrs Ferguson, Mr Broxburn's sister, has just arrived in this country from Canada,' I explained. 'She cannot remain here indefinitely.'

'I understand. But is the estate of a size to require a formal submission?'

At that time, estates of less than £13,000 could be dealt with over the counter by the sheriff clerk, using a procedure which entailed little more than filling out a form. I explained that Jim Broxburn's deposit book had never been made up. After interest and the values of his gun, van and chattels had been added, the estate might well exceed that sum.

'I understand your difficulty.' The sheriff asked Mrs Ferguson a few questions. In a low, clear voice she confirmed her identity and stated that she had been the late

67

Jim Broxburn's only close relative and that as far as was known he had left no will. She had had the forethought to bring her birth certificate.

The sheriff returned his attention to me. 'A Bond of Caution will be needed. Mrs Ferguson being resident abroad, will that present any difficulty?'

'No, M'lud,' I said. I had spoken to my usual insurers that morning. They had quibbled but had ultimately agreed to furnish a bond.

The sheriff considered in silence, frowning gravely. He was a fair and kindly man, but he hated to be hurried and, for the best of reasons, I was asking him to act many times more quickly than is normal in an executry. 'The petition appears reasonable,' he said. 'But I am given to understand that Mr Broxburn did not die a natural death.'

For the first time, Sergeant Fuller's intransigence proved to be an advantage. 'I believe, M'lud, that the police are satisfied that the death was accidental,' I said. That much was truth. I preferred to forget that I might well be forced to argue the contrary, in Alexander Deeley's interest.

'I see.' The sheriff turned back to Mrs Ferguson, asked for her passport and studied it. 'Whatever the outcome of the deliberations of the police,' he said, 'I note that Mrs Ferguson had not been in this country for several years until today and is therefore hardly likely to have any culpability.'

He studied the ceiling tiles for a moment before proceeding. 'We should allow a little time in case a will should be found or another claimant come forward. I shall consider afresh on Monday, at which time perhaps I might be advised of the progress of the police enquiries and whether the fiscal intends to call for an inquiry. In the meantime, a search must be made for a will. Mr Enterkin,

I think that we should give you some official standing. I appoint you *vitious intromitter*.'

'I'm grateful, M'lud.'

Mrs Ferguson was waiting by the door when I left the courtroom having gathered my belongings. I apologised for keeping her waiting.

'That's OK,' she said. 'I guess you've been roasting that damn fool and telling him it was his own fault?'

'Good guess,' I said.

'Anyone could see that he'd've got off lighter if he'd pled guilty from the start.'

We took a short-cut through the hotel and walked along the Square to the office. Mentally, I was kicking myself. I should have foreseen that an early hearing of the petition might result in the police being forced to report before Keith had had time to complete his parallel investigation.

Miss Jelks looked up as we came in and smiled. Mrs Ferguson seemed to have made a favourable impression.

'You found him, then?'

'Just where you said.'

I broke in before they could get round to my habit of snatching brief repose when nothing else required my attention. 'Would you phone around?' I said to Miss Jelks. 'Find out whether Jim Broxburn left a will with his bank manager or with some other solicitor.'

I took Mrs Ferguson into my inner sanctum. Its air of well-worn antiquity usually pleased me, but I suddenly wished that it projected a more swinging image.

She settled herself lightly in the client's chair. 'Now,' she said. 'Tell me how Jim died, please. Was it really some sort of an accident?'

'Before I go into that,' I said, 'you tell me one thing. I take it that your brother made no contribution to your support?'

She managed a tired smile. A rather attractive dimple made a momentary appearance. 'Chuck – my husband – pulls down a good salary. He's an associate professor at a university. And I write fiction for the magazines. How could a bakery worker need to make me an allowance? We could have helped him out if he'd needed it, but he never did. He always said that he could make out. Why do you ask?'

'It's a rather complex story,' I said. I told her as much as I knew about her brother's death. She listened silently and intently, a frown gradually rippling her smooth brow. 'The police seem satisfied that he was laying poison for predators, contrary to the Wildlife and Countryside Act nineteen eighty-one. They may suggest that he was doing so as an employee and under the instructions of Mr Deeley, who is already my client.'

She was wide awake now and I could see indignation coming. I hurried on. 'I never knew your brother, but from what I'm told he would be the last person to do such a thing. But the evidence already seems incontrovertible and it's quite possible that more may turn up – while, on the other hand, the only alternative supposition would seem to be that somebody – '

'Knocked him off?' she asked.

'Well, yes. You don't seem shocked.'

'I'm shocked that he's dead. The how and why seems less relevant. Go on,' she said.

It took me a few seconds to gather up my thoughts again. 'If the facts should turn out to be as the police suggest, and if you were in any way relying on your brother for support, you might have had grounds for a suit against Mr Deeley, in which case I couldn't act for you.'

She rubbed her eyes. 'I'm jet-lagged to hell,' she said, 'but I can't see that we've got a problem. One, just as you said, Jim would never do such a thing and I'm not going to stand up in court and swear that he would. I've a whole stack of his letters at home which I've kept because he wrote from the heart about the Scottish wildlife. Made me homesick sometimes. I was born not far from here. In one of his letters, I remember, he estimated how many gamebird chicks he was losing to hawks. It wasn't a whole lot, he said. And then he wrote how he was getting around it, like using scarers and making sure that there was a good supply of easy meat for them.'

'That's not exactly cast-iron evidence,' I pointed out. 'People can suddenly act out of character if they're pushed too far.'

'It's good enough for me. Second, I didn't depend on Jim for a thing. And, thirdly, I still have friends around here. I phoned one of them after you called me, wanting to know who I was dealing with. She gave you a clean bill and now that I've met you I can see that she wasn't mistaken. You'll do whatever's right.'

I mumbled some thanks. Such accolades rarely come to a solicitor.

'Listen,' she said. 'Seems to me that Jim's death needs investigating and, if the police have already made up their minds, they're going to call it a day. Could I hire you to look into it?'

'You'd do much better to hire Keith Calder,' I said, 'if he'd take it on.'

Her eyes, which had been half closing again with tiredness, snapped open. 'I've heard of him. Jim sent me a clipping once. Isn't he some sort of a private eye?'

'Don't let him hear you say so,' I said. 'He's a gunsmith and he knows the countryside better than most keepers. But he's a nosy devil and once he gets his teeth into a mystery he never lets go. I think that he's already looking into it for Mr Deeley.'

'Your Mr Deeley will only be interested in getting his own head off the block. I want to know what happened. Jim seemed to think a lot of this Mr Calder. Can you introduce me to him?'

'Very easily.' I remembered that Keith was working without what I would consider to be a proper fee. 'He may prove rather expensive.'

She shrugged. 'What the hell? As I told you, we're not short. I wasn't expecting anything from Jim's pools win and I don't need it. Let some or all of the money go to clearing his name.' She yawned, stretching her arms above her head in a manner which I found disturbing. 'I must go eat and sleep,' she said. 'Then I won't come over quite so stupid. Would you take me out there and introduce me around in the morning?'

The next day would be Saturday, my favourite morning for pottering around the office and moving things from where Miss Jelks, in her fetish for tidiness, had put them and returning them to where I could be certain of finding them again. 'I may not be free,' I said, 'in which case I'll delegate that duty to Keith Calder. I'll be in touch.'

I saw her to the door. 'I'd like to see your brother's letters,' I said.

She yawned again and then looked at a small watch. 'I'll be phoning Chuck later, once I'm sure he's up,' she said. 'I'll tell him to put them in the mail.'

I hesitated before putting one last question. 'In his letters, did he mention a lady friend?'

Mrs Ferguson was not in the least coy. 'Not in so many words,' she said. 'But I wrote to him once that it was high time he was married. When he wrote back, he didn't refer directly to what I'd said but he wrote that he wasn't going short of anything. I was in no doubt about what he meant. I guessed that she had to be a married woman, because

72

if she'd been single he'd have said something about her, wouldn't he?'

I made an almost fruitless visit to the police. Sergeant Fuller was unavailable. I saw his immediate superior, an elderly inspector coasting towards retirement. He refused to give me access to the photographs of the death scene or other evidence, but he did at least promise that no evidence of any kind, however obscure its relevance, would be discarded without consultation.

I managed to get in an hour or two on useful and profitable work that afternoon before turning my mind again to the death of Jim Broxburn. I tried to phone Keith, first at the shop and then at Briesland House. But Keith, it seemed, had gone off on his own and nobody knew where. I left messages asking him to call me back.

Keith often disappears into limbo but he is rarely out of touch. When Miss Jelks put an incoming call through to me a few minutes later I fully expected it to be Keith but it was Alexander Deeley.

'The police have been here again,' he said. 'That sergeant and another one. I refused to make any statement until you were present – '

'Quite right,' I said.

' – but they were ominous – '

'They can be good at that.'

'Don't interrupt, there's a good chap,' he said, more gently, perhaps, than I deserved. 'They said that they'd be back tomorrow morning and when I said that I could hardly expect my solicitor to come all the way out here on a Saturday morning they asked whether I'd prefer to discuss the matter at their headquarters – which, as they pointed out several times, is only about a hundred yards from your office. It still sounded like an invitation to "help the police with their enquiries".'

73

I was becoming ever more convinced that Jim Broxburn had been driven by the predation on his beloved pheasant chicks to the point of forgetting his principles and laying poisoned bait. If he had survived the result of his clumsiness, a prosecution might well have succeeded. To prove Alexander Deeley's complicity would be considerably more difficult. But Deeley sounded perturbed and there are times when a solicitor feels obliged to keep his client's spirits up.

'Don't let them get you off-balance,' I said. 'When the police are at their most ominous it's sometimes a last-ditch attempt to force an error. What time did they say that they would be there?'

'About eleven.'

It could have been worse. The police sometimes keep unconscionably early hours. 'I'll be there,' I said. 'Mrs Ferguson – Broxburn's sister – flew in from Canada this morning. I'll bring her with me.'

Mr Deeley's mood improved. His voice went from worried to peevish. 'It's all very inconvenient,' he said. 'Mr Calder's coming out to visit the traps for me again tomorrow, but I'm already supposed to be directing a working party of the syndicate members and also giving a hand with the silage. An extra driver saves a lot of time at silage cutting. Oh well, I suppose if I can be in two places at once I should be able to manage three.'

'They may not keep us for very long,' I said.

We disconnected.

While we spoke, Miss Jelks, hatted and coated, had put her head around the door, given me her farewell sign and mouthed that she would see me on Monday.

I pottered for a little longer, restoring disorder where it was to be preferred, and then headed for the hotel. Penny was doing an evening stint and when she was on duty I usually took a bar meal there. We were meticulous about those meals being paid for, but she was not above slipping me a generous portion or an extra vegetable.

I had planned to leave a message for Mrs Ferguson but hers was the first face to catch my eye when I walked into the lounge bar. She was seated alone at a small table and tucking into a steak pie. A glass of the house wine was beside her plate.

Penny took my order for another steak pie and dispensed two more glasses of wine. I carried them over to Mrs Ferguson's table and put one of the glasses down.

'Hello there,' she said. 'Come and join me. Is that for me?' She had changed her clothes and looked fresher but mildly stunned. Her hair, which earlier had been neatly but severely pulled back, had been given a few deft touches into a more becoming style.

I sat down and pushed the spare wineglass across. 'To help you sleep,' I said.

She produced her appealing smile, complete with dimples. 'I don't need help, but thanks for the kind thought. I slept for an hour and then hunger woke me up again. Those damn airlines reckon that as long as you don't quite starve to death they've done all right by you. Unless you go first class, that is, but I grudge being ripped off for that much extra fare in exchange for another three inches of seat and twice as much rubber food. Next time, I guess I'll take sandwiches and a flask. After this, I'll sleep ten or twelve hours and be right as rain. So what's new?'

'I have to go to Ladyhill Woods tomorrow morning,' I said. 'One of our local detective sergeants is making threatening noises at Mr Deeley. So I'll be pleased to take you. If you have a hired car, perhaps you'd like to drive?'

'I didn't fancy learning to drive on the left again,' she said. 'Not in a strange car and propping my eyes open on matchsticks. I took a car with a driver and sent it back.'

'In that case, I'll pick you up,' I said. 'Between ten and ten-thirty?'

'That'll be fine.'

Penny brought my steak pie and picked up Mrs Ferguson's empty plate. My helping seemed moderate but I made no complaint. Nor did I introduce the two ladies. My understanding with Penny is that when she is on duty we may or may not know each other, depending on the company.

'I haven't been able to reach Keith Calder yet,' I told Mrs Ferguson. 'But I gather that he'll be at Ladyhill Woods tomorrow. You can meet him there.'

'Right.' She finished her second glass of wine and muffled a yawn. 'Time I got back into the sack,' she said. 'Hunger won't wake me again. Nothing will for the next twelve hours, short of the Last Trump. Even for Gabriel, I don't know that I'll bother.'

She pushed back her chair. I rose to my feet, which brought more faces into view among the gathering throng of Friday evening sippers. 'Stay awake for a minute or two longer,' I said. 'Keith's just walked in.'

He saw me wave and brought his small whisky over to join us. I performed an introduction. Most of us are in difficulties when introduced to the bereaved of somebody we never knew, but Keith, who is seldom if ever flummoxed, murmured just the right words before turning to me. 'I got your message,' he said, 'so I made an educated guess and tracked you down.'

'Don't let that give you an exaggerated idea of his abilities as a detective,' I told Mrs Ferguson. 'I often eat here. Keith, I was going to invite you to meet Mrs Ferguson and perhaps to drive her out to Ladyhill Woods tomorrow.'

'Delighted,' Keith said. 'I'm going out there early.'

'I'm going out a little later. The police have been

upsetting Mr Deeley and they're seeing him at eleven.'

'I think I'd prefer the later start,' Mrs Ferguson said. 'I've some sleep to catch up on. What do you suppose the police want?'

'At a guess,' Keith said, 'they've had the reports of the pathologist and the analyst and they've found something pretty deadly in the way of agricultural chemicals.'

Mrs Ferguson was looking almost haggard with tiredness but her chin went up. 'Could be,' she said. 'But even so, I won't believe that Jim was laying poison for birds of prey.'

'No,' Keith said. 'He wasn't.'

A silence fell over our table so that the babble of talk around us flooded in. 'The evidence looks pretty damning,' I said at last.

'But it's flawed. I'll tell you something. As I was leaving home after lunch I crossed with Mrs Chegwin in that big estate car she drives. I guessed that she'd be going to see Molly – my wife,' he explained to Mrs Ferguson. 'They can't stand each other but they both go in for wildlife photography, which gives them some common ground. Mrs Chegwin only has a cupboard for a darkroom. No sinks. When she wants to do enlargements at home, she has to carry in basins of water. Molly has a proper set-up and a much better enlarger, so Mrs Chegwin pockets her principles and scrounges the use of Molly's facilities.

'I went on as far as the shop to tell Wallace that I wasn't coming, if that doesn't sound too Irish, and I doubled back home and sneaked into the house the back way. I could hear somebody in the darkroom and Molly in the kitchen, so I knew that I was right. I had to stay hidden until the old biddy had finished her printing. Then she and Molly sat down to tea and scandal while the prints dried and I sneaked into the darkroom and ran off another set from her negatives. I have them here.' He

77

patted his pocket. 'That's why you couldn't reach me.'

After a moment's thought I decided that theft of a photographic image was not a crime and that the laws of copyright were unlikely to apply if there was no intent to publish. 'Well done,' I said. 'Can we see them?'

'Certainly.' Keith looked round. The room was becoming crowded. 'But not in here.'

'We could go up to my room,' Mrs Ferguson said. 'Please. Anything, if it gets me one step nearer to my bed. And Mr Calder, would you care to work for me on this?'

'I already am working on it, for Mr Deeley.'

'But all you're trying to do for him is to keep him out of trouble. You could do that by showing that he didn't know what the hell my brother was getting up to. I want to know what happened, good news or bad. Finding that out for me wouldn't stop you keeping Mr Deeley's head out of the wringer, right? How much would you charge?'

Keith smiled. He had a very charming smile when he cared to use it – or so the ladies always seemed to find it. 'Not too much,' he said. 'I'm already getting a sort of a fee from Alec Deeley. If Ralph's acting for you I'll agree it with him. No result, no fee.'

'That seems fair,' Mrs Ferguson said. 'Now, I can't keep my eyes open much longer. Let's go.'

I could feel Penny's eyes on my back as we left the bar.

The hotel is more than a hundred years old. The proprietors had kept the décor fresh without losing the Victorian dignity. Mrs Ferguson's room was spacious and comfortable, deeply carpeted and heavily curtained. The only modern intrusions were an attached bathroom, an intercom and a large television.

'You're sure that you want to see these?' Keith asked Mrs Ferguson. 'They're not the sort of photographs I would usually show to a bereaved relative.'

'Quite sure. I'm tougher than I look.'

There was only one chair. We found it easiest to sit on the bed and spread Keith's black-and-white prints across the duvet. He pushed aside some photographs of birds. 'It was easier to print the lot than to try to select the right negatives,' he said. 'These are the ones we want.'

Mrs Chegwin had done a thorough and, to my unskilled eye, a very competent job. If she had approached the task with any squeamishness it had not caused her hand to shake.

The same thought had occurred to Keith. 'Infirm of purpose, give me the camera,' he said. 'There's a touch of Lady Macbeth in the vision of Mrs Chegwin coolly photographing a dead gamekeeper in the hope of compromising an enemy.'

Mrs Chegwin had taken a dozen shots and, although some of these were virtual duplicates, the scene was fully covered. Jim Broxburn's body lay face down with the head turned to one side. The face was invisible in most of the shots, which was a mercy – death by respiratory inhibition does not leave a pleasant aftermath. Mrs Ferguson was visibly shaken but braced herself to continue.

A small hypodermic syringe, looking very much like the one with which my doctor had given me inoculations prior to the last occasion when Penny and I had holidayed abroad, was beside the dead right hand and near to it was a small bottle containing what seemed to be a murky liquid. In the background, a very ordinary-looking shotgun lay across a stump.

Several exposures had been devoted to the left hand of the corpse which held, or lay on top of, a small, dead bird. The puncture wound, emphasised by a dried droplet of blood, showed clearly on the web between the thumb and first finger.

'It still looks damning to me,' I said. 'What do you see that's new?'

'These photographs are informative in a way that the old bat never intended.' Keith looked at Mrs Ferguson. 'Even if I hadn't been told that your brother shot from his left shoulder, I'd know it now.'

'How?' I asked him.

'For God's sake use your eyes,' Keith said. He tapped a long shot of the body which showed the gun, muzzle towards the camera, in the foreground. 'That gun's got cast-on instead of cast-off. If you shot it off the right shoulder you'd miss away to the left. Can't you see it?'

I hadn't the faintest idea what he was talking about, so I just nodded.

'Can you confirm that your brother was caurry-fisted?' Keith asked. 'Left-handed, I mean. Not ambidextrous?'

'I do remember what caurry-fisted means. Jim was a diehard southpaw from a boy,' Mrs Ferguson said.

'That doesn't mean very much,' I protested. 'He had two things to bring together, one in each hand. If he already had the bird in his left hand he might well not have bothered to change hands. It might even account for a degree of clumsiness,' I added.

Keith nodded impatiently. 'But first he had to fill the syringe.'

'True,' I said, 'but – '

'He'd do that with his dominant hand.'

'And put the bottle down beside the other, which is where it is,' I pointed out.

'This is interesting,' Mrs Ferguson said, 'but I'm out on my feet. Will you two please get out of here and let me get to bed? You can fill me in tomorrow.'

'But – ' I said again.

'Just look at the position of the bottle,' Keith said. 'He had to put that down. He couldn't hold the bottle

80

and the bird and a syringe all at the same time. If he was standing when he jabbed himself, which isn't likely, and he fell forward, you'd expect the bottle to be near his feet. If he'd knelt down to use the ground as his table, which is what most men would do, the bottle would have ended up beside his thigh. Try it. Kneel down on the carpet.'

'I'll take your word for it,' I said.

'I want to get to bed,' Mrs Ferguson said plaintively. She got to her feet and stood swaying.

'And there's another thing,' said Keith. 'More than one, in fact.'

'What?'

'You're both married men,' Mrs Ferguson said. 'I don't suppose I've got anything you haven't seen before. Would one of you unzip me please?'

'If you look closely,' Keith said, 'the bottle and the syringe are both almost full. Ralph, I think that the pathologist should be asked to estimate what volume of solution at that concentration had been injected. We could then – '

Mrs Ferguson had managed to unzip herself. She began to struggle out of her dress. We got out of there in a hurry, leaving the photographs scattered across the bed.

SIX

Penny, at my invitation, again exchanged shifts with her friend Lucy and came with us to Ladyhill Woods. The invitation had been accepted more spontaneously than it had been proffered. Penny, after seeing me eat with a lady whom she described as attractive and then disappear in the direction of the bedrooms, had left me in no doubt that any failure to welcome her company would be taken amiss.

'I did not find her attractive,' I said. 'She's too skinny. And Keith was with us the whole time. You don't have to come and play gooseberry.'

'Whenever did Keith's presence make anything respectable?' Penny retorted. 'I prefer the word chaperon. Do you really think that she's skinny? You don't think that I'm getting too fat?'

'Not fat,' I said. 'Plump. Pleasantly so.'

'Look who's talking! You should have more sense than to expose yourself to gossip at your age,' she said more cheerfully. 'I know that I can trust you. I've known that for several years.'

The fact that we had been married for nearly twenty years turned her last sentence from a compliment into a knife in the ribs but I refused to let her see that it had struck home. Penny was revealing a streak of jealousy which had hitherto been unsuspected. (Keith, I learned later, had headed straight for the bar when we parted company and had been startled or amused enough to mention to a friend the means by which Mrs Ferguson had driven us out of her room. The story had come to Penny's ears.)

Mrs Ferguson, when we collected her from the hotel, looked at Penny in a faintly puzzled way, as if wondering where they had met before; but she accepted the presence of my wife as chauffeuse, adviser and chaperon without comment. Refreshed by a good sleep and breakfast she had recovered some sparkle and I could begin to see why Penny had suspected her of being attractive. The fine weather was returning at full strength and the two of them chatted guardedly about it all the way to Ladyhill Woods.

When we emerged from the tunnel of trees on to the sunny sweep of gravel, I saw that Sergeant Fuller's car had again pre-empted the most desirable parking place. Somebody was sitting in it but the darkened windows reduced them to a vague shape. Two men were sitting under the tree and Alexander Deeley was nervously pacing the gravel.

As we got out of the car he was already speaking to me, ignoring the ladies. 'Sergeant Fuller's here already and he's brought a constable to take notes.'

'That would be normal. Has he said anything informative?' I asked.

'I refused to discuss anything until you were here. Keith Calder arrived hours ago. He was going to do one small job for me, but he's had time to do that and to go round the traps more than once. I don't know where the hell he's got to.'

'You have me,' I said, 'and that's more than enough. Mrs Ferguson, Jim's sister, has come out with us – ' they nodded to each other ' – but introductions can wait. While we talk to the Sergeant, the most useful thing for the ladies to do would be to go through Mr Broxburn's cottage. Don't remove anything,' I told Mrs Ferguson but with a meaning glance at Penny, 'but you could start separating everything into categories. Useful documents; whatever you'd like to keep; what you think should be sold; and what can be thrown away. Above all, look for a will.'

'Surely,' Mrs Ferguson said. 'And Mr Calder woke me early this morning with the phone. Doesn't that guy ever sleep?'

'Quite often,' I said. 'It's his friends who don't always get the chance.'

'I believe you. If you see him, tell him that I spoke to Chuck again. I just caught him before he went to bed. And Mr Calder was dead right.'

Alexander Deeley had been almost hopping from foot to foot with impatience during this exchange. 'If you want refreshments or anything else,' he said rapidly, 'you'll find my wife in the house. She has the key of the cottage. We can meet properly later on. Let's get this over,' he said to me. 'I have two other matters screaming for my attention. It would have been three except that Mr Calder kindly went after starlings with an airgun last night and he brought me a supply to keep that sparrowhawk occupied.'

Neither policeman bothered to rise at our approach, nor did Sergeant Fuller introduce his companion. Instead, the Sergeant came straight to the point before we were settled in our chairs.

'Is Mr Deeley now prepared to answer our questions?'

'That might depend on the questions,' I said.

The Sergeant pursed his lips and looked constipated for a moment. 'Very well,' he said. 'I may as well begin by telling you that we have the pathologist's report. Mr Broxburn died from the effects of alpha-chloralose poisoning. A sample of his blood, together with the syringe,

85

the bottle and the dead bird were sent for analysis. The analyst detected alpha-chloralose in the bottle and the syringe.'

'And in the body?' I said.

The Sergeant looked less sure of himself. 'Chloral hydrate, which I understand is much the same thing.'

'Thank you for the information,' I said. One of Keith's comments suddenly made sense to me. 'Did the pathologist give an estimate as to the quantity injected into Mr Broxburn? And into the bird?'

The Sergeant looked at me sharply. 'If he did, he didn't include it in his report.'

'The question should be asked,' I said, 'and the answer should be compared with the amounts missing from the syringe and the bottle.'

He shrugged. 'I can ask the questions,' he said. He looked at Mr Deeley. 'Do you still deny that Mr Broxburn was laying poisoned bait for birds?'

'Don't answer,' I said quickly. 'Mr Deeley has no way of being sure what the syndicate's unpaid, part-time gamekeeper was doing at the time of his death; and if, which we do not admit, Mr Broxburn was laying poisoned bait, Mr Deeley would not know whether it was laid for birds. I may say that we are conducting our own investigation. This is far from complete and, unlike yourself, we are not prepared to comment further until we have reached a conclusion.'

'But we have reached a conclusion,' the Sergeant said. 'In the face of all the evidence, are you not prepared to accept it?' He sounded almost plaintive.

'No,' I said. 'Other interpretations are possible.'

'What other interpretations?'

The Sergeant and Alexander Deeley were watching me expectantly. Even the constable looked up from his notebook.

Keith could no doubt have produced a dozen other interpretations, but he had a devious mind and an intimate knowledge of rural matters. The only alternative theory which occurred to me entailed some other person offering to help with the poisoning of the bait and deliberately injecting Mr Broxburn as he held the bird. But that hypothesis, while it might transform the death from accident to murder and give an avenue of escape from the Health and Safety at Work Act, would entail an admission that Broxburn had set out to poison birds of prey. I wished to God that Keith had kept me apprised of his deliberations, but that was never his way.

'No comment until we have finished our enquiries,' I said.

The Sergeant looked at Mr Deeley and gave a small shrug, as though drawing Deeley's attention to what a broken reed his legal adviser was proving.

'Do you still deny giving Broxburn any instructions regarding the use of poisons?' he asked.

Deeley opened his mouth.

'Don't answer that question,' I said urgently. 'It's loaded.' A negative answer, in the event of a court finding that Jim Broxburn had indeed been laying poisoned bait as Deeley's agent, could have precluded any defence against a charge, under the Health and Safety at Work Act, that he had not been given proper instruction in the safe handling of toxic material.

The Sergeant bit his lip for a moment. He had my qualified sympathy. A silent suspect presents a problem. He could bring Mr Deeley before a sheriff – either after charging him, for which he was by no means ready, or by having him cited as a Crown witness to give a precognition on oath. As an alternative, he could put some more cards on the table.

To my relief, he chose the latter course. 'You may

care to know,' he told Deeley, 'that a witness has come forward who overheard you instructing Broxburn to poison sparrowhawks.'

'He's lying,' Deeley said – before I could intervene, even if I had wanted to. 'No such discussion ever took place.'

'You deny it?'

'Absolutely.'

It would be best, I decided, to dispose of this development before it became accepted as fact. Alexander Deeley had not yet been cautioned, but a court might well allow answers given in the presence of his legal adviser to be used in evidence. 'Are you questioning my client as a future witness at the Fatal Accident Enquiry? Or as somebody suspected of involvement in an offence?'

The Sergeant only hesitated for a second. 'As a witness,' he said.

'Then you have no intention of bringing a charge against him?'

'I didn't say that.'

'But you haven't cautioned him,' I pointed out.

The Sergeant hesitated again and then rattled off the words of the formal caution. 'And now can we proceed?' he asked.

'Possibly,' I said. 'But if you seriously suspect my client of breaking the law, I must advise him to say no more until we know the grounds on which you suspect him. This may hamper your enquiries into Jim Broxburn's death, but we can't help that.'

Sergeant Fuller looked at me in irritation. 'What are you after?' he asked me.

'I think that my client has a right to be confronted by this witness,' I said.

'Not a legal right,' the Sergeant said.

'A moral one. Or, if that doesn't carry any weight with

88

you, consider the waste of time and resources if you proceed on the unsubstantiated word of a witness who is, at best, mistaken. You must have expected this,' I added. 'Your witness is surely the person sitting in your car. If we can dispose of this aspect right away, we may be able to be more helpful.'

The Sergeant looked at his companion. 'Fetch Mrs Chegwin,' he said. The constable dropped his pen, stretched cramped fingers, rose and walked towards the cars.

Alexander Deeley had tensed up at Mrs Chegwin's name. I saw his knuckles whiten and noticed that the Sergeant was watching him closely. But Deeley, with a visible effort, managed to keep his voice calm although his words were forceful. 'If you believe anything that woman says about me, you've got to be either gullible or mad. She's hated my guts for years and she believes whatever she wants to believe.'

'Even if that were true, it wouldn't necessarily make her wrong this time,' Fuller said.

Mrs Chegwin tripped across the grass with the self-satisfied air, quite out of keeping with her middle-aged robustness, of a young bride dragging a prize catch to the altar. The Sergeant rose but Deeley and I pretended to be unaware of her. There were only four chairs so the constable was left to stand and manage his notebook as best he could.

'Now,' said the Sergeant when they were settled, 'Mrs Chegwin. I'd like you to repeat what you told me yesterday.'

'All of it?'

'About the conversation which you overheard. Try to remember the exact words.'

'Very well.' For an instant Mrs Chegwin speared Alexander Deeley with a glance of triumph. She took a deep breath which was answered by a faint squeak of overstressed nylon. 'It was on Tuesday. I was in my garden, rooting out some couch-grass from among the rock-plants, when I heard voices among the trees beyond the hedge.'

'You know the area she's referring to?' the Sergeant asked Mr Deeley.

Deeley nodded.

The Sergeant returned his eyes to Mrs Chegwin. 'You recognised the voices?'

'They were Mr Deeley and Mr Broxburn. I'd have recognised them anyway, but I was expecting them. One particular hen pheasant had raised a brood among the brambles just beyond my garden – such a sweet creature, I don't know how anybody could bear to shoot them! – and a sparrowhawk had come across the field from Gled Corner and it had killed and half eaten one of the chicks. A shame, but nature must be served and I got a wonderful photograph of the moment of the kill.

'Mr Broxburn had a feeding hopper and a water-dispenser – '

'Drinker,' Deeley said.

' – a drinker in the wood and I knew that he'd see the poor little dead bird when he came to refill them and I was curious to know how he'd react. Evidently he'd fetched Mr Deeley. I heard him say something about "You can see for yourself".

'I heard them moving around, looking at the evidence, and then Mr Deeley lowered his voice and he said, "Well, you know what to do, and the sooner the better. A dose of the right stuff should fix the beggar. Isn't science wonderful?"' She gave Mr Deeley another look of Virtue Avenged and then fell silent, looking at her fingertips.

'Well?' said the Sergeant.

Deeley looked at me. 'I have an answer,' he said.

In every case there comes a moment when you have to show at least some of your hand. The Sergeant's proof was growing stronger by the minute and if Alexander Deeley did not make an answer now he would soon find himself doing so before the sheriff. 'Give it,' I told him.

He met the Sergeant's eye squarely. 'As far as I know we haven't lost any birds to sparrowhawks this year. What Broxburn had been showing me was an outbreak of what's called gapes. It's caused by parasitical worms in the windpipes. It stunts the birds and kills some of them. What I was telling him to do was to get hold of some Wormex to mix with the feed. This . . . this harpy's story was correct except in one detail. I wouldn't have said "beggar". I said "beggars". Plural.'

'That shouldn't be difficult to prove,' the Sergeant said. 'The Wormex should be in the feeder.'

Deeley looked uncertain. 'He went off to his work shortly after that and he died soon after coming off work the next morning. The stuff comes in a bottle big enough to treat five hundred pheasants and costing around thirty quid. He probably intended to phone around his keeper friends to see whether one of them had some to spare or wanted to share a supply. I don't think he'd have had time to do anything about it.' He looked concerned. 'I've been assuming so. I certainly hope that he hadn't time to add any to the feed in the hopper. It mustn't be used for more than twenty-four hours at a time or it does more harm than good. Mr Calder brought some Wormex with him this morning and he was going to deal with it for me.'

Sergeant Fuller sat silent while he weighed Deeley's answer. 'So we'll have to depend on Mr Calder's opinion?' he said at last.

'Very glib,' Mrs Chegwin said suddenly. 'What does this . . . this "gapes" look like?'

'I don't have to answer your questions,' Deeley said. 'I'd like to know,' the Sergeant said. 'If you don't tell me, I can ask the first keeper I meet. And I can always take a look in your wood for myself.'

Deeley shrugged. 'It's common knowledge,' he said. 'I just don't like being cross-examined by that person. The birds seem to be yawning.'

'We can go up there and see whether the birds still look bored,' Fuller said to nobody in particular.

'That wouldn't prove a thing,' Mrs Chegwin said furiously. 'His birds could be yawning their heads off but I still heard him talking about the sparrowhawk. I remember now. He used the word "beggar" – in fact, I think that he used a ruder word – but that was earlier. What he said was "A dose of the right stuff should fix that . . . predator".'

Silence fell. Mrs Chegwin glared defiantly round the table. Her correction had been punctuated by the hesitations and vocal fadings of a liar who is being forced to improvise. My face probably showed disbelief, as Deeley's certainly did. Even the Sergeant seemed to have doubts.

The risk was that, now that Mrs Chegwin had been shown the weakness in her story, she might have time to 'remember' a better one. 'While you look at the gapes, you could also look for the corpse of the pheasant chick,' I pointed out.

Mrs Chegwin drew herself up and protruded her formidable bosom. 'That was probably the bird which Broxburn was using to put down his filthy poison,' she said.

The Sergeant shook his head. 'That bird wasn't half-eaten. Look at your own photographs if you're in any doubt.'

'Well, I know what I heard and I'll repeat it in court any time you like. And I hope you get jailed,' she added to Deeley in a vicious undertone.

'Impossible,' I said. 'In the almost inconceivable event of a conviction, the penalty would be a fine. There's no provision in the law for a custodial sentence.'

'Then there should be.' Mrs Chegwin got to her feet so abruptly that her chair fell over. 'It's legalised murder,' she said. She stamped away across the grass.

The Sergeant watched her go with indecision written all over his face. 'You wouldn't care to tell me why she hates you so much?' he asked Mr Deeley.

'Why do you want to know?' I asked.

'Because we have two flatly contradictory stories from two people who are obviously at daggers drawn. There's little room for errors or misunderstandings. One is lying to get himself out of trouble or else the other is lying from spite. The physical evidence may sort them out or it may not. I want to know who I'm dealing with.'

I decided that what he really wanted to know was which one of the two was the more likely to blow up under cross-examination.

Deeley was looking a question at me. 'Think,' I said. 'Could it be taken as reflecting unfavourably on you?'

'Not by any thinking person,' Deeley said slowly. 'In fact, I'd like to tell it. It may not only give the Sergeant an insight into Mrs Chegwin and me, but his reaction might give us an insight into him. You can shout if I'm putting my foot in it.

'It happened a little more than a year ago. Not that we'd been friendly before that, but at least we'd been polite and avoided open warfare. Our views were diametrically opposed but we managed to avoid each other or to meet without discussing anything more contentious than the songbirds.

'Magpies were nesting in the next wood above Gled Corner. People tend to like magpies – they're colourful and they look cheerful and perky. But they're nasty

93

brutes. There's a plague of them in Britain just now, although we seem to be missing the worst of it. Their favourite prey in the spring is the eggs and nestlings of other birds and when they're feeding young of their own they can clear quite a large territory. Quite apart from the syndicate's gamebirds, I enjoy as much as the next man having songbirds around.

'I knew roughly where the nest was but I couldn't get at it, so I took out a gun and tucked myself into hiding on their favourite flight-line, but without any luck. I knew that I was well hidden, yet something seemed to be spooking them. So I climbed out of the ditch and took a look around. That . . . that ogress was in the field about twenty yards away, waving her arms whenever they approached. I asked her nicely to go away and let me get on with my legitimate business on my own land but all I got in return was abuse. I told her about the habits of magpies and she called me a liar.

'There's no future in arguing with bigots. I went away, but I sneaked back the same evening and got both of them. And Jim Broxburn climbed the tree for me, to make sure that we weren't leaving any nestlings to starve; but there were only two eggs and they were already cold.

'While we were doing that, she came screeching at me again. We both tried to convince her that it had been in the best interest of wildlife generally, but even when I showed her a blackbird chick which one of the magpies had been carrying she insisted that I must have stolen it out of the nest and put it there.

'She complained to the RSPB, among others, but the only result of that was a phone-call to me from one of the RSPB's directors explaining rather delicately that although she was a member of that body they did not necessarily associate themselves with her every word. I asked him to write to me to that effect but he wouldn't do it. I didn't really expect him to, but it was worth a try.'

We sat while the Sergeant cogitated, in silence except for the song of a bird in the tree above us. It sounded very much like the bird which had been singing there two days earlier.

'Any comment?' Sergeant Fuller said suddenly.

The constable jumped. The question had been addressed to him. 'It's truth about pyats,' he said.

'About what?'

'About magpies. I've seen 'em.' The constable was broadly spoken.

The Sergeant got to his feet. 'Show me some gapes,' he said to Mr Deeley. 'Can we walk it from here?'

'Easily,' said Deeley. 'Let's go now before that Gorgon has time to tamper with the evidence.' He gave a little cough of nervous laughter. 'I'll tell you this. There are usually a few dead chicks around at this time of year. If we find one which is half-eaten, I'll want an odontologist to compare the marks in it with Mrs Chegwin's revolting gnashers. Are you coming with us, Mr Enterkin?'

Ignorant as I might be about country sports, I had noticed that in shooting territory the coverts are always on the tops of whatever hills are available. This, Keith had explained, was so that birds could be sent over the guns high and therefore difficult. I had earned his contempt by observing that anybody who was so determined to render something more difficult than it naturally was would no doubt make love standing up in a hammock.

'You don't need me,' I said hastily. 'Just stick to the subject and defer answering any other questions until we've spoken again. I'd better go and see whether the ladies have turned up a will or some more assets.'

Deeley only nodded and the three prepared to walk off. One advantage of the ageing process is that laziness may be put down to failing health, while if you exhibit the least energy anyone but a wife will probably say, 'Isn't he wonderful for his age?' Youth seldom benefits from such compassion.

I made in the direction of Broxburn's cottage but at the corner of the house I met Keith. 'Mrs Ferguson phoned her husband,' I told him, 'and you were right. Right about what?'

'I knew that that had to be it,' he said. 'Listen, you'd better come and meet Fergus. The old fouter knows something but it's against his principles to talk unless he's forced or bribed, on top of which he's so hung over that he's barely alive. I'm told that he drinks his entire pay-packet on Friday nights and then lives out the week on what he can catch or pick around the farm – the occasional rabbit plus any vegetable from kale to turnips. They say that he even eats raw sugar-beet. But he's good with animals and works hard when he's sober.'

'Shouldn't we wait until he's recovered?'

Keith shook his head emphatically. 'Catch him while he's weakened,' he said. 'He's the sort that the more he has his wits about him the more he lies or acts stupid, because it's him against the rest of the world. He's up in his caravan now.'

That word 'up' again. 'Can we take a car?' I asked.

'Not necessary. It's only a step. Come on.'

I gave in ungraciously. I refused to gallop to keep up with him so he shortened his stride to match mine. From behind the cottages another farm track led around the end of the barn. As we walked, he subjected me to intensive questioning. I gave him a brief summary of my dealings with Sergeant Fuller and described the contents of the cottage in some detail. The story of Mrs Chegwin seemed to amuse him.

'Had the worm stuff been added to the pheasant feed?' I asked him when he had run out of questions.

'No. I've done it. If I'm free, I'll come back tomorrow and put out fresh pellets and grain.'

Another, more important, question had to be asked. 'How much do you intend to soak my client for all this gadding about?' I asked him.

'We'll talk about it later. We won't quarrel.'

'Now, just a minute,' I said. I halted and looked around for a seat but there was nothing to be seen on which I would have trusted the seat of one of my better suits. 'I don't usually look gift horses in the mouth, but when you come bearing gifts you're worse than the Greeks. Why are you putting in so much time on a matter which seems to be comparatively trivial?'

'You think so? Don't stop walking or we'll never get there.'

We started walking again, more slowly. 'Yes, I do think so,' I said. 'If the police were taking it seriously, there'd be more than a sergeant on it. I don't think they can make a case against Alexander Deeley, and the Health and Safety Executive are probably waiting to see which way the police go. Mrs Ferguson's concern for her dead brother's reputation may be understandable but I wouldn't expect you to throw yourself into it unless financially motivated. Twenty years ago I might have suspected that you were trying to ingratiate yourself with the lady, but you keep telling me that you've turned over more than one new leaf since then. Do you know something I don't know?'

My question was open to an insulting retort. He restrained himself but he also avoided a direct answer. 'I'll tell you something,' he said. 'We have a good scene in this country, but it's being fouled by a class hatred which is at least a hundred years out of date. We have a landscape which has been managed, or at least influenced, by sporting needs for centuries and is very much the better for it. We have a legal system which adjusts the seasons

97

or gives protection to a species if it's in any danger. The system doesn't always work in the favour of sport – curlew, redshank and Brent geese are three prime examples – but in general, and as long as everybody plays ball, it works well. Shooting interests do more than any other to keep the wildlife scene healthy, whatever you may hear from the propagandists in the media.

'But that isn't how the public tends to see it. Our opponents distort the truth or even produce damned lies and the public believes them. To the townsman, it "stands to reason" that shooting is cruel and harmful to wildlife. If I've learned one thing in life,' Keith said irritably, 'it's that anything which is said to "stand to reason" doesn't stand up at all and that anything which "goes without saying" would be better left unsaid.'

'Come to the point,' I suggested.

'I thought that I had. The point is that this relationship with public opinion is delicate. The huge benefit that the countryside reaps from fieldsports goes unnoticed, but any bad behaviour on our side gets maximum publicity. It sometimes – very rarely – happens that a keeper loses patience with seeing his carefully nurtured charges preyed on by raptors which, in his view, are a hell of a long way from being endangered. When there's a prosecution, it creates a barrier around the argument that keepered land is the richest in wildlife. At this delicate time, when we're at the mercy of every idiot from the Brussels bureaucrats to the police anti-gun lobby, I'm damned if I'm going to let another scandal brew up out of something that didn't happen.'

Nothing is ever gained by debating fieldsports ethos with Keith, especially when his blood is up. He seemed to be suggesting that Jim Broxburn had been murdered. Or perhaps there was some other comparatively innocent explanation for his death. Too direct a question would probably only push him further in the direction of obfuscation.

'How can you be so sure that it didn't happen?' I asked him. 'And what was the other thing you were going to tell us last night after looking at Mrs Chegwin's photographs?'

'Oh, that! Didn't you notice anything about the dead bird?'

'It was dead,' I said. 'And it was a bird. If you tell me that it was a young pheasant I'll believe you. Where is this caravan?'

'That's it up ahead.'

The caravan seemed to be a tiny speck miles ahead and high above us and I said so.

'Nonsense,' Keith said briskly. 'I'll give you something else to think about, to keep your mind off the Long March. You didn't notice the bird's neck? The damn thing looked like an embryo ostrich. A keeper doesn't have to wring the neck of a healthy bird if he wants one to use as bait. God knows young pheasants are suicidal enough. They drown themselves or get hung up in wire or chilled overnight or peck each other to death. But, anyway, if a keeper was going to lay bait for a sparrowhawk it'd be because the hawk was killing pheasant poults. And they don't usually carry them off; they tear at them on the ground where they made the kill and then come back for another meal at the same place and the same time next day. The keeper would lay his poison there, preferably in the previous day's kill.'

'He mightn't have been after a sparrowhawk.'

'He wasn't,' Keith said.

'What I mean is that he might have been after some other bird of prey. Eagles carry off their prey, don't they?'

'Not around here. If there's an eagle in the wild

within a hundred miles, it's a vagrant on passage.'

I thought of mentioning the eagle which had escaped from Mr McAngel's premises. But we were arriving at our objective and, becoming tired of being wrong, I was glad to drop the subject.

I had been spurred onward by the thought of a comfortable seat in the caravan, but that was not to be. The caravan itself looked sound and almost respectable but conditions in and around it would have reduced the most sluttish housekeeper to tears. I could see several gutted rabbits hanging inside in a cloud of flies and more flies were being attracted to a small pile of rotting vegetable matter near the towbar. The site was pretty, backed by a stand of silver birch trees and with a view across the fields to the rising moors, but the smell in the vicinity suggested that the great outdoors was preferred to use of the chemical toilet.

The caravan's occupant, who was sitting in the doorway nursing a mug of tea and a severe case of what seemed to be alcohol poisoning, had evidently slept rough and in clothes which he had not changed since last working in them. Fergus – if he had another name I never heard it – was about my own considerable age but thin and wiry. His grey hair had been cut so crudely that it stood straight out from his head. He was in dire need of a shave and this, combined with unwashed and pallid skin, gave him the look of death; and yet, beneath the symptoms of the alcoholic drop-out, I could see the blurred features of what had once been a proper man. Cleaned up and dried out, I could see him taking a modest but responsible place in the world.

The small plot of waste ground was separated from the field by a dry-stone wall. I took a seat on one of the larger stones and blotted my face and neck with a handkerchief. The heat was returning.

'Good morning,' I said.

Fergus's reddened eyes looked at me without pleasure and then switched to Keith. 'You again,' he said.

'This is Mr Deeley's lawyer,' Keith said. 'If you won't talk to me you can talk to him.'

'Gar him gang awa',' Fergus said thickly.

'Not until you've told me what you know,' I said.

Fergus looked into his mug and muttered something unintelligible.

'Mr Deeley needs my help and I need yours,' I said.

Fergus lifted one buttock and expelled some wind.

It went against my humanitarian instincts to bully a man who was so obviously paying for his folly, but I steeled myself. 'You can talk to me or you can talk to the sheriff,' I said.

'I'm wabbit,' Fergus said. He was lapsing into broad Scots in order to put an extra barrier, in the way of communication, I was sure.

'I'm tired too,' I said. 'We're all tired. Tell me what you know – '

' – about Wednesday morning,' Keith put in.

' – about Wednesday morning and you can go back to sleep.'

'I maun gae tae my work,' Fergus said.

'You usually take most if not all of Saturday off,' Keith said. 'You work Sundays instead.'

'Who does this caravan belong to?' I asked.

'It's mine,' Fergus said.

Keith gave a snort of laughter and shook his head at me.

'Start getting it cleaned up for the next man,' I said. 'Mr Deeley won't want to keep you on if you can't speak the truth when he needs it most. I'll be back with a policeman to take you in front of the sheriff.' Fergus stayed dumb. Life had inured him to threats of dismissal or of the law. But he was of the type to whom legal papers are awesome

101

and doom-laden portents of disaster. 'I'm going to serve a citation on you,' I said.

'There's nae ca' for ony o' that,' Fergus said suddenly. 'Whit is't you're efter?'

I looked at Keith.

'You were out early on Wednesday morning?' Keith said.

'Aye.'

'While I was looking for Mr Broxburn's traps, I came across a few wire snares. Were they yours?'

'Aye.'

'You visited your snares before you went to your work?'

'Aye.'

'This is like pulling teeth,' Keith said in an aside. 'Fergus, while you were going round your snares on Wednesday morning, did you see Mr Broxburn or anybody else?'

Fergus fell silent. I thought that he had dried up again but it seemed that he was only thinking. 'Aye,' he said at last. 'It was athort twa fields, mind, hyne-awa'. I saw a mannie that I thought must be Jim Broxburn, speiring at ane o' his traps abune Gled Corner. A whilie later I saw twa men gaein' back doon the hill together and ane o' them was stoiterin' as if he'd taken a dram and the other was giein' him a hand. That's a' that I could see and nae damned papers can mak' me say that I seed ony mair.'

'You didn't recognise either of them?' I asked.

Fergus grunted a negative.

'Was either of them carrying a shotgun?' Keith asked. 'Or both?'

'Neither o' them,' Fergus said.

'And they were above Gled Corner?'

'Aye. And now, awa' tae hell wi' the baith o' you.' He got unsteadily to his feet.

'Wait!' Keith snapped, so suddenly that I jumped. Fergus froze in the caravan's doorway. 'What else is there? What haven't we asked you that we should?'

Fergus sneered at him. 'That's no' for the likes o' me to tell the likes o' you.'

'But you saw something else, later?'

Fergus paused and then nodded, very slowly. 'Twa guns by the side o' the track, back up the hill. Ane was Jim's old twelve-bore.'

'And the other?'

'A wee gun wi' just the yin barrel. Looked like a four-ten.' Without another word Fergus climbed into the caravan and shut the door.

'That'll do for the moment,' Keith said. 'That's all we'll get out of him just now. We can always find him again. When he's dried out, the promise of a bottle might open his mouth a little wider. Come on.'

He turned away. I thought that he was looking remarkably satisfied with a discussion which had revealed very little about even less. I heaved myself to my feet and set off after him. 'Why were you quizzing him about shotguns?' I asked.

'Broxburn would have set off carrying his gun. A keeper never knows when he'll get a shot at a carrion crow or a fox. His gun was beside him when he was found. Somebody must have gone back to fetch it.'

'I don't see that it matters. Jim Broxburn wasn't shot.'

'He could have been,' Keith said.

'He could have been, but he wasn't.'

'If you say so,' Keith said in tones of great patience.

SEVEN

Thinking over what Fergus had said and what Keith had and had not said, I forgot to be tired until we were almost back at the farm. More and more, Keith seemed to be demonstrating that Jim Broxburn had been murdered.

'It sounds to me as though he'd caught a poacher,' I said at last. 'From a distance, one man constraining another could look very much as Fergus described them.'

'But then how do you explain Broxburn's death?' Keith demanded. 'Do you think that he stopped off at Gled Corner and asked the man to help him put down poisoned bait? He'd be laying himself open to blackmail.'

Out of my ignorance of matters rural, I had been content to leave all theorising to Keith, certain from experience that he would suddenly produce an explanation that was not only satisfactory but self-evidently true. But now I was visited by sudden inspiration.

'He found somebody else laying poisoned bait,' I said, 'and he was hauling him down to the house to phone the police. He didn't realise that the man had a syringe of poison ready for use in a safe container or palmed. The man suddenly took it out and jabbed him in the hand and then set the scene to look as though Broxburn had been doing just what he'd been preparing to do himself.'

Keith was looking amused. I expected him to pour scorn on my thinking but, as so often, he had a surprise for me. 'Well done,' he said. 'It isn't what happened but you've come part of the way along the right track.'

'Carry me the rest of the way.'

'I don't know the rest yet.'

'I meant the rest of the way back to the house,' I said.

'Take off a couple of stone and then ask me again.'

'Which bits did I get right?' I asked humbly.

'None of them. The bits were wrong. Only the direction was right. I'll give you something else to think about. Alpha-chloralose in the body turns into chloral hydrate, but death wouldn't be instantaneous. Chloral hydrate's what they used to use for knockout drops. I asked one of the doctors at the hospital. The first symptoms would be sleepiness, mental confusion and unsteadiness followed by respiratory failure. You see what I'm getting at?'

'When Fergus saw them, Jim Broxburn was already dying?'

'That's how it looks to me,' Keith said. 'Dying, and perhaps he didn't even know it.'

I found the concept – of being within minutes of death and unaware of it – to be disturbing but, when I said so, Keith only snorted at me. 'Best way to go,' he said. 'Fear of death must be worse than death itself. That's one thing that does stand to reason.'

If I had not needed all my energy for putting one foot before the other, I might have scratched my head. Keith's suggestion was that somebody had been helping Jim Broxburn towards his cottage or the big house, perhaps seeking medical aid. But when Broxburn had collapsed and died, the same somebody or another had set the scene for an accident. If there had indeed been a murder, would the murderer have behaved so irrationally? Or was there a hidden logic behind the movements?'

106

When we rounded the corner of the barn, Penny and Mrs Ferguson were crossing the paddock towards the house. They turned and came back to meet us and Penny handed me the large key.

'We've done as much as we can for the moment,' she said. 'And Mrs Deeley came a few minutes ago to say that there would be some lunch on the lawn.' She looked at me closely. 'And you look as if you're due for a service,' she added. 'You'd better come and sit down and cool off.'

We set off across the paddock and round the end of the house.

'I think that somebody's been through the place,' Mrs Ferguson said.

'The police,' I said. 'And me.'

She shook her head. 'Somebody else,' she said firmly. 'Unless you came straight from the chicken house? Jim was very fussy about his floors, so he always changed his boots for slippers and brushed himself down at the front door; but I noticed a feather on his sitting-room carpet, almost under the chair.'

'The farm manager, who lives next door, said something about an intruder,' I told her. 'He heard a door slam in the wind and feet going away. I took him to mean that the intruder didn't get inside.'

'It seems that he got as far as the sitting room,' Keith said. 'What sort of feather was it?'

'I put it in my purse,' Mrs Ferguson said. 'I was sure you'd want to see it.'

On the table under the tree stood a jug of iced lemonade and four glasses. Beside them, an inverted glass bowl was covering a large plateful of sandwiches. The Deeleys, plus any lingering members of the working party, were leaving us to lunch in privacy. I subsided into one of the white chairs with a groan which was mostly of pleasure. I dislike sandwich meals but the exercise had given me an appetite.

'There's a whole stack of letters to Ann,' Penny said when we were seated and the sandwiches had been passed round. 'Mr Broxburn kept copies of all the letters he wrote by using a piece of carbon paper and writing heavily with a ballpoint. And he's kept all her letters to him. Somebody should go through them. I only dipped into one or two, with Ann's permission, but they seem to give a clear picture of his life.'

'There's no sign of my last letter to him,' Mrs Ferguson said. 'It had an enclosure from Chuck. It must have got here by now, however crazy the mail's getting to be.'

'I think that it was still in his pocket,' I said.

'I found something even more interesting. An insurance policy,' Mrs Ferguson said. 'One of those endowment-cum-life policies. The beneficiary is a Mrs Celia Farrow.'

'Lucky Mrs Farrow,' Keith said. 'Is it for a large sum?'

'Only three thousand pounds,' Mrs Ferguson said. 'Not a big sum these days.'

I emptied my mouth. 'Is it a policy with or without profits?' I asked.

'With.'

'Is it new?'

'It had been running for a few years,' she said.

'Then it could be worth more than its nominal value,' I pointed out. 'I'd better take a look at it.'

'Before you get over-excited,' Keith said, 'bear in mind that a man with eleven thousand in the bank wouldn't fake up his own suicide to look like an accident for the sake of a much smaller sum.'

I had indeed been considering the possible implications of a suicide clause, but Keith's comment made sense.

108

'Who is this Mrs Farrow?' I asked. 'Did your brother ever mention her in his letters?'

Mrs Ferguson shook her head. 'Not by name. She must have been the mysterious lady friend.'

For once, Penny did not have the answer at her fingertips. 'I'll find out,' she said. She jumped to her feet – very lightly, considering – and walked towards the house, still nibbling at a sandwich.

'May I see that feather?' Keith said.

From her purse, Mrs Ferguson produced a tiny feather, cream in colour but with a very dark shading at the tip. 'To me, it looks to be any old feather, like out of a pillow or something.'

With great care, Keith stowed the small feather away in his wallet. 'I'd be interested to see the pillow that this feather came out of,' he said.

Penny returned in a minute or two, bringing with her a tray with mugs of coffee. We cleared a space on the table. 'Mrs Farrow lives further up the valley,' she said, 'next door to that man McAngel. I'm told that she's the one who does all the real work around his falcons. She lives with her husband,' she added pointedly.

'She could still be the mysterious girlfriend,' Keith said. 'Doing a Lady Chatterley.'

'Of course she could,' Penny said. 'Almost certainly she is. Or was. The affair's over now and we don't want to make trouble between husband and wife.'

'Discretion called for,' I said. 'There are ways of conveying a legacy to a spouse without the other spouse knowing. These things arise from time to time. I'd better go and call on the lady. If the husband's at home, I can make some excuse and withdraw.'

'He probably won't be,' Penny said. 'He's a partner in a business and he travels a lot.'

'I'll come with you,' Keith said. 'I've been looking

for an excuse to call on Mr McAngel. If the husband's at home, we can say that we wanted to look at the falcons. It'll be a fine leg-stretch for us.' He winked at Penny.

'You can walk if you want to,' I said. 'I've used up this year's ration of wear and tear. My legs are trailing along the ground behind me. I'm taking the car.'

'He's pulling your leg,' Penny said, soothingly but with mirth in her voice. 'Your face was a picture! Take the car. Ann and I can wait here.'

'I'm going with them,' Mrs Ferguson said. 'If this Mrs Farrow was my brother's mistress, I want to meet her. Reading between the lines of his letters, she made the last few years special.'

'Then I'll just stretch out on the grass and have a snooze,' Penny said. 'Three of you will be enough for the poor woman to cope with.'

I was unwilling to curl up among the dog-hair in the back of Keith's jeep, nor would it have been reasonable to expect Mrs Ferguson to do so. Despite Keith's protest that it would be quicker to walk, we got into the Rover and I drove back to the road and followed it northward up the floor of the valley.

The steep, tree-hung sides of the valley closed in around us. Ahead, rising towards the moors, were green fields dotted with animals which, at this distance, looked strangely lithe for cattle or sheep. I was saved from making another gaffe by a sign at the mouth of a gravel road which read 'Ladyhill Deer Farm'. Our road twisted away around the last of the trees and petered out in front of a cluster of buildings, set back from the road beyond a dry-stone wall.

Central to these was what had evidently been a sixteenth-century peel – a fortified tower built in the bad old days of the Border reivers, when a combination of wars and royal policy had resulted in total lawlessness on both sides of the Border. It was in poor condition, the roof gone and the upper stonework beginning to crumble, but the solid oak door, which stood ajar, showed the glint of a modern lock.

To the right of the peel as we looked, and so close as to be almost attached to it, stood what seemed to have been the original farmhouse. This had been a rambling building, but only part of it had been preserved and cleverly restored to make a house of modest size and stern character. The remainder had been taken down to knee level and incorporated into the layout of a simple garden of grass and shrubs and small, scattered trees. On the other side of the tower and set further back, another house had been made from a stone barn of rather later date. This garden, like the other, had been laid out so as to require little attention other than an occasional pass with a mower but, in the context of those buildings and the troublous times from which they dated, floral beds would have looked like mere frivolity.

In a basket chair near the door of the tower a woman was seated. She had a card table in front of her on which she was attending to a variety of leatherwork, some of it quite elaborate, which I assumed to be connected in some way with the hawks. Several perches in the form of hoops or posts stood in the shade of trees and on two of these two birds were tethered. They glared at us with angry eyes as we got out of the car.

The woman ceased her work and waited impassively as we entered through an iron gate. She was in her later thirties. Her features were strong without being unfeminine. Even seated, she could be seen to be above average height; and her casual dress of jeans and a man's shirt, with her dull red hair cropped carelessly short, could not disguise an overall picture of allure. Some women, a

111

precious few, need no ornamentation but exude sexuality as if through the pores. If she set her mind to it, this woman could have lured a priest out of his hole.

At the moment, she was not setting her mind to any such enticement. She watched our approach in a cold silence. Keith and Mrs Ferguson had fallen behind me. I introduced myself and Mrs Ferguson. 'You're Mrs Farrow?' I asked.

'I am.' She looked past us, eyebrows slightly raised.

'Don't mind me,' Keith said. He produced his most charming smile, the one which, according to Penny, made a high percentage of female knees turn into Plasticine. 'I only came for the ride. I wanted to see the falcons.'

'Help yourself,' she said. 'Those are the only two here at the moment. There's a fieldsports fair on somewhere and Stuart McAngel's putting on a show.'

'Thank you.' Keith strolled off in the direction of the larger bird, a savage-looking creature, slate-blue above with paler underparts, barred legs and a dark moustache. Its feet and lower legs were a gaudy yellow.

'Is Mr Farrow at home?' I asked.

'Did you want him?'

'On the contrary,' I said. 'We wanted to speak with you on a matter which you might prefer to keep confidential.'

'Now's your chance. My husband's a partner in the deer farm and he's away setting up a veniburger marquee at the same game fair. I don't expect either of them back until some time tomorrow. Is it about Jim Broxburn? I was expecting you or somebody like you, but not so soon.'

There was only one chair and she was firmly in occupation of it, so Mrs Ferguson and I were forced to stand like culprits before the desk of a headmistress or a female magistrate. Keith, I noticed, after a short wander on the grass, had seated himself beside the nearer hawk, well within earshot. I would not willingly have placed myself within striking distance of that beak or those talons, but Keith always had a remarkable knack of making friends with wild creatures. The bird was already reconciled to his presence and Keith seemed to be engaged in grooming its feathers with a twig, to its considerable pleasure.

'Perhaps I'm jumping the gun a trifle,' I began in explanation, 'but Mrs Ferguson was Jim Broxburn's sister and she's only come over on a short visit. There's an application before the sheriff for her appointment as executor and I expect it to be considered on Monday. She has already asked me to deal with her brother's estate on her behalf.'

Mrs Farrow's face went from bland disdain to a frown. 'Did Jim's will not name an executor?'

'We haven't found a will,' I said. 'He seems to have died intestate.'

Her eyes flicked to Mrs Ferguson and back to me. 'Jim always intended to make me his beneficiary,' she said flatly.

I suppressed a sigh. This conversation was taking a line that I had followed many times before. 'I expect that he did have that intention. But people never expect to die until they're very old – if then – and they keep putting off making a will. The general philosophy seems to be that "If I can't take it with me I'm not going to go." A laudable ambition but not many achieve it.' There was not the least flicker of expression at my little joke. I hurried on, made unaccountably nervous by her manner. 'Mr Broxburn did make some provision for you. He took out an insurance policy in your name. You should benefit to the tune of several thousand pounds. I can arrange for the money to reach you without your husband's knowledge, if you so wish.'

'That's all very well,' Mrs Farrow said coldly. 'I've no

secrets from Arthur. I was a very good wife to him until – for medical reasons which are none of your damned business – he lost interest in that side of marriage. After that, he didn't mind my taking up with Jim Broxburn, just as long as we were discreet about it and he got his meals on time. Jim used to leave his van tucked out of sight and walk up here whenever Arthur was going to be away overnight. I knew about that policy, but it's a drop in the ocean compared to his pools win.'

'Which he shared with five colleagues,' I pointed out.

'It does seem unfair,' Mrs Ferguson said impulsively. 'It was very remiss of Jim not to make a will. He said very little in his letters, but I knew that there was a woman in his life who made him happy. I wanted to meet you and thank you. From the moment that I found that policy . . . '

I had seen enough of Ann Ferguson to know that she had a warm heart. She was about to make some gesture towards sharing the estate. One of a solicitor's duties is to restrain a client from impetuous generosity which might be regretted at leisure. I opened my mouth to interrupt but Mrs Farrow beat me to it.

'You did *what*?' Her voice rose and her frown had become a glare as imperious as that of the two hawks. She switched it to me and I could feel the heat of it. 'Did you let a relative go poking through Jim's papers? No bloody wonder you haven't found a will!'

I felt my scalp prickle. This had the signs of trouble. 'There was another person present throughout,' I said.

Mrs Ferguson had turned scarlet. 'That's a terrible thing to suggest!' She turned and backed towards Mrs Farrow, raising her arms. 'You can search me if you like.'

'You wouldn't have it on you,' Mrs Farrow retorted. 'Take your bum out of my face.' She lifted the card table out of her way and got to her feet. In keeping with all her words and gestures, the movement was controlled, confident and aggressive, almost contemptuous. Upright, she was seen to be nearly six feet tall.

'I'm coming down to Jim's cottage with you. That's where I want to search. And I shall have something to say to the sheriff on Monday. Wait right there while I put the birds indoors. We sometimes get boys with airguns coming around and I'm responsible for them until Stuart McAngel comes back.'

She took up a gauntlet which had been lying beside her chair and pulled it on. Releasing the straps – jesses, Keith later said that they were called – which restrained the first hawk, she transferred it to her gloved wrist. Keith, without benefit of a gauntlet, took up the other and followed her through the door of the peel. I would not have cared to have those talons around my wrist, but with Keith the bird was docile.

'Don't look at the décor,' Mrs Farrow's voice came muffled through the doorway, spiced by an echoing from the stone walls. 'No matter how often we whitewash the place, the soot comes through.' Like the hawks, she seemed to have decided that Keith was her only friend among us.

'What condition is the tower in above the ground-floor vault?' Keith asked curiously.

'Terrible. The floors are hanging. Only the strands of dry rot are holding them up. We wouldn't dare to use the ground floor if it wasn't for the stone vault.' They emerged into the sunshine and she locked the door carefully. 'Are you going to drive me down to the cottage?' she asked. 'Or do I have to walk?'

Greatly though I would have enjoyed telling her to walk, it seemed politic to offer her a lift. She took the front seat in the car, as of right.

The journey began in a silence which reeked of hostility. I searched desperately for something to say which would be innocuous and remote from the question of Jim Broxburn's estate, just to clear the air and prevent the pressure from building any further.

'Did you say soot?' was the best I could manage. 'Why would the stonework be sooty?' I tried to make my voice sound curious and friendly but it only sounded timid.

'God knows,' Mrs Farrow said without interest. 'Cooking fires, I suppose, when the place was under siege.'

'Uh-uh,' Keith said. 'In those days, if you went to visit a neighbour and found the place empty, it was usual to blow up his peel so that you could catch him with his breeks down next time you came to call. Such behaviour wasn't considered unneighbourly – it was the understood thing. So, if you were going on a raid and leaving your buildings unguarded, one precaution was to fill the ground floor of the peel with smouldering peat. It tended to discourage the neighbours from visiting with kegs of gunpowder.'

'It would do that,' Mrs Farrow said in a friendlier tone than I had heard her use. 'You live and learn.'

The Sergeant's car had departed, so I parked in the shade in front of the big house. We disembarked.

'The key of the cottage,' Mrs Farrow said. I hesitated. 'Come on,' she said impatiently. 'It may pay you to waste time, but I have things to do.'

'I don't think that it would be any more proper for you to be alone in the cottage than for Mrs Ferguson,' I said. 'Less so, in fact.' I had no desire to spend an hour or two cooped up in a small cottage with an angry lady who also resented my supervision. If Mrs Ferguson undertook the duty, there would be blood and hair under the fingernails within an hour. I looked round for Penny. 'Perhaps . . . '

116

Mrs Farrow began to assume her furious look again. Keith jumped in quickly. 'I'd be happy to lend my company,' he said.

Immediately, Mrs Farrow looked happier. It occurred to me that she would be in the market for a new lover now that Jim Broxburn was seeking his pleasures among the angels; and Keith was still an attractive man with an eye for the ladies. He adored his family but it was a well-kept secret that I had several times had to intervene when his departures from the straight and narrow path of virtue had left him open to blackmail or litigation.

Keith took the large key from me and the two went off, almost hand in hand. My jacket, relieved of the weight, began to return towards its original shape but my mind was still heavy. It seemed that, on top of having to keep Alexander Deeley out of trouble while guarding my own back, I must be prepared to drive a wedge between Keith and Mrs Farrow if need be.

We walked towards the chairs under the tree and found Penny sleeping on a rug in the shade. She roused as we approached and tried to tidy her hair with her fingers. 'How did it go?' she asked.

'Not too well,' I said. I took her hands and helped her to her feet. I felt better already. For one thing, her influence over Keith was immense.

'That awful woman!' said Mrs Ferguson.

'Mrs Chegwin?' said Penny.

'Mrs Farrow,' I said. 'A different woman but just as awful in her own way.'

The white chairs under the tree were beginning to seem like a second home. When we were settled, Mrs Ferguson burst out again. 'The bitch! Would you believe, she thinks I found a will and tore it up?'

'Or so she says,' I put in.

'Says?'

117

I was back on familiar ground. Executry is a fertile area for fraud. 'She may know very well that there wasn't a will. But she might be able to convince a court that there had been one – if, for instance, she could produce witnesses who swore, truly or falsely, that they'd witnessed your brother's signature on it.'

'Would anybody go that far for a few grand?'

'People have gone much further for much less,' I told her. 'What seems a trivial sum to you may seem like the wealth of the Incas to somebody who's being blackmailed or pressed to settle a debt, or who's set their heart on something just beyond their means.' I looked at Penny. 'Could you swear that you were together all the time?'

'Easily,' Penny said.

Mrs Ferguson put a hand on Penny's arm. The two seemed to have become bosom buddies within an hour or two. 'That's good of you,' she said, 'but you know it wouldn't be true. While I went through Jim's papers you were in the bedroom, checking that there was nothing in the pockets of his clothes.

'Cheer up,' she added in my direction. 'We'll win through. And, if we don't, what the hell? It's only money.' If I looked upset it was more at the realisation of Penny's willingness to commit perjury than at the possible damage to my reputation and Mrs Ferguson's inheritance. Even so, her last sentence struck me as mildly blasphemous.

I had heard the sound of a tractor heading into the farmyard. Now Alec Deeley came out of the house bearing a welcome tray of his eternal iced lemonade. I decided that he must have it delivered by tanker. He took the fourth chair.

'The working party's putting down fresh straw in the feeding rides,' he said, 'but they've got enough to keep

118

them going for the moment so I can take a breather. I'll take them up another jug when I go back.'

'Did you show the Sergeant a case of gapes?' I asked him.

'I did indeed. I had a horrid suspicion at first that the gapes would have cleared up overnight, the way the tooth stops hurting when you get to the dentist.'

'Or your car goes quiet when you try to let the mechanic hear the noise the motor's making,' Mrs Ferguson said.

'Exactly. The few pheasants around seemed healthy and I could almost see the Sergeant's suspicions sprouting like weeds. But then we came across a group of three, standing around and yawning. I never expected to be relieved to see a case of the gapes, but that's what I felt at that moment. I think he was satisfied. And there was no sign that a sparrowhawk had killed a poult there.' He looked at Mrs Ferguson. 'Mrs Chegwin – '

'The other "awful woman",' I reminded her.

' – is doing her damnedest to prove that your brother was laying poison for sparrowhawks on my orders. She claims that she can back up her accusation with a photograph of a sparrowhawk killing a poult just beyond her hedge. The Sergeant hunted for what seemed like an hour but there was no corpse and only the few feathers that one might expect.'

'Now, that's very interesting,' Mrs Ferguson said. She opened her bag. 'I have the photographs that Mr Calder left behind yesterday evening. They're prints of the whole film which included the shots Mrs Chegwin took of my brother's body. Mr Calder – '

'I don't think that you need say any more about how he came by them,' I put in. The less said about some of Keith's methods, the better.

'OK, if you say so. Anyway, there were also a few shots of birds. I guess they'd have been on the film

119

before she found poor Jim.' She handed him the packet of prints. 'You take a look,' she said. 'I just don't care to see those shots of his body again.'

Mr Deeley scanned rapidly through the photographs, tutting over the views of the body. 'Here we are,' he said. 'Peewits in flight. Geese on grass. A pheasant sitting on eggs. Just one shot of a female sparrowhawk just as she . . . ' His voice tailed off. He looked at Mrs Ferguson and then at me, decided that neither of us was likely to be conversant with the Scottish countryside and held out the enlargement to Penny. For a second the photograph was almost under my nose. Mrs Chegwin had captured a moment of total savagery and frozen it for ever. Each detail was needle sharp, from the feathers in the half-folded wings to the glare in the raptor's eye. I felt a shiver for the unlucky prey.

Deeley had no pity to spare for the chick. 'The kill is happening on thin grass,' he said. 'But what would you say that shrub was, in the top corner?'

'Wild broom,' Penny said. 'It's slightly out of focus but you can tell.'

'That's what I thought. And there's no broom growing wild within a mile of her house.' He slapped his fist into his other palm and began to rise. 'I'm going to go and see that harridan – '

'If you do that, she'll change her story again,' I said. 'She may even think of a better one. Leave it to me. Let her try to tell that tale in front of a sheriff. She can crawl out along the limb before I saw it off.'

He settled back into his chair and nodded without making any other reply, but there was a smile in his eyes and I knew that he would take my advice.

'And now,' Penny said, 'I think that we must go. The hotel is expecting me.'

Mrs Ferguson nodded suddenly. 'I just knew I'd seen

you before,' she said. 'Can you make a good Manhattan?'

'The best,' Penny said, smiling.

'That's what I fancy tonight. And shake one for yourself.'

We got up to go, some more stiffly than others. 'Keith's in the keeper's cottage with Mrs Farrow,' I said to Mr Deeley. 'I'd better see him. And he wants to tell you something about the Wormex.'

'I'll walk round with you. Then I must go back to the working party. Fergus will have loaded the trailer again by now.' At the mention of Fergus, the memory of the caravan and the condition of its occupant came back to me. Deeley glanced at me and he must have read something of my thoughts. 'Don't think too badly of the old chap. He and his wife used to occupy what's now the keeper's cottage. You couldn't have wished to meet a neater and more God-fearing couple. They kept the place like a new pin and the garden would have looked good at the Chelsea Flower Show. After his wife died, Fergus went to pieces. I do what I can for him, which isn't much; but he's still a good worker and he's welcome to a job for as long as he wants it. God willing, something will happen to snap him out of it one of these days.'

Penny and Mrs Ferguson paused at the corner of the house. Deeley and I walked on but we were only entering the paddock when Keith and Mrs Farrow emerged from the cottage and came in our direction. The atmosphere between them seemed much less friendly than before. I was relieved to note that Keith, if he had ever had a chance of acquiring Mrs Farrow as another mistress, had just, in the modern vernacular, blown it.

Keith showed no signs of a broken heart. He grinned at Mrs Ferguson. 'The letter you told me about hasn't turned up yet,' he said. 'And there's no sign that he ever made a will.'

Mrs Farrow walked straight at me and slapped the big key into my hand so hard that it bruised the ball of my thumb. 'I haven't finished yet,' she told me. 'But I have to go now. I'm expecting a phone-call. I'll be back at ten tomorrow morning and I'll expect you, personally, to let me in.'

Without giving me a chance to say that we don't all get what we expect out of life, especially from me at what was virtually crack of dawn for a Sunday morning, she turned and walked off.

'I could give you a lift home,' Keith said after her.

'I can walk.'

Mr Deeley raised his eyebrows at Keith. 'What's got up her nose?' he asked.

Keith chuckled. 'She has one of those acquisitive noses. Despite several strong hints, I stayed behind her shoulder like an evil genie. Whatever she read, I read, which she seemed to find inhibiting – except that once, when she thought I was still there, she looked round and found that I wasn't. You'd have thought she'd be pleased, but after that our romance seemed to be over. The lady is up to something. For one thing, she searched everywhere except in the one area which I'd have expected her to make a bee-line for. I think that somebody should sleep in there tonight.'

'I'll do it,' Deeley said. He took the key out of my unresisting fingers. 'I can get by on a few hours catnap. It'll give my wife the chance of a good night's sleep.'

I nodded, to give the arrangement my official blessing. I wanted to ask Keith about the letter that Mrs Ferguson had told him about and which he had taken such care to mention in front of Mrs Farrow, but I was tired and no doubt all would be revealed in time. 'Penny was right,' I said. 'We must go.'

Keith looked at his watch. 'So must I,' he said. 'But

I'll be back early in the morning. There's something in the cottage I want to find and Mrs Farrow as good as told me where to look for it. I'll pick you up around eight, Ralph.'

The idea of leaving home at eight on Sunday or any other morning was high on my list of activities to be avoided. 'You don't need me,' I said. 'You have my authority, such as it is, to search. For a will, of course.'

'Of course. Make your own way, then, but be here by ten to let the lady in. After that you can delegate the supervision of her to me, if you like, and go back to bed.'

EIGHT

There may be country solicitors who leap out of bed at the crack of dawn and arrive in the office before any client could possibly expect their attention, but I have never been one of their number. A lifetime in legal practice has accustomed me to a leisurely pace in the mornings and an even longer lie-in on the Sabbath.

It was therefore with some reluctance that I dragged myself creaking out of my bed and hobbled downstairs. Even the Lord's Day can have ungodly hours and this was one of them. But I had allowed time for a good breakfast and I was on the now familiar road soon after nine. The day was fine again but close and humid, with a dark haze on the horizon. I was alone. Penny had allocated the day for housekeeping while Mrs Ferguson intended to hire a taxi and to visit the scenes of her youth and the grave of her parents.

It still lacked some minutes to ten o'clock when I arrived at Alec Deeley's house. Keith's jeep had stolen the only patch of shade, but the sun would move round. I parked close behind and smiled to myself. Movement had loosened my joints but the heat was oppressive. I took my time circling the house and crossing the paddock.

Outside the pair of cottages, a tractor and trailer were parked and idle beside Jim Broxburn's van. I found Keith and Mr Deeley conversing in earnest whispers just inside

125

the door. Keith put a finger to his lips. 'Keep it down,' he said. 'Next door is full of ears and things have been happening.'

'I have eyes in my head,' I said softly. The small hallway was lit by a row of glass panes beside the door and one of these, close to the lock, was now obscured by a rectangle of brown paper.

'Oldest trick in the book,' Keith said. 'Treacle and brown paper. You can break the pane almost silently and there's no tinkle of falling glass.'

'I was sleeping in the armchair with the hall door open,' Deeley said. 'A small sound woke me. I must have made a noise, because whoever it was ran off.'

'Cursing his luck or his clumsiness,' Keith said. 'For the second time. Interesting, isn't it?'

'Very. Have you only just got here?' I asked him.

Keith uttered a single bark which was intended to express mirth. 'I've been here for hours. While Alec went for a shave and a freshen up, I did a search of my own. Nothing's been removed,' he added, seeing my expression. 'But you'd better take charge of this.' He handed me a sealed envelope. His signature and that of Alexander Deeley were scrawled across the flap. It seemed to contain papers and something soft, perhaps a small scrap of cloth.

'What is it?' I asked him.

'It's what Mrs Farrow is looking for. I'm afraid you won't get back to your bed just yet.'

'I wasn't going to,' I said indignantly. Perhaps I could snatch a doze on the lawn while Keith and Mrs Farrow were in the cottage.

Keith knocked that idea on the head immediately. 'You'll have to stand guard over her,' he said. 'There's something I want to take a look at. Could you detach the lady from her keys?'

'No,' I said firmly, 'I could not. I'm getting enough stick from her already. Tomorrow, she's going to accuse me of conniving at the suppression of a will. And you can't go breaking into people's houses. Any evidence you obtained would be inadmissible.'

'I only want to look inside the peel.'

'You've already seen inside the peel.'

'I want to look again. I'll lurk outside the cottage door. All you have to do is to get her to leave her handbag behind when she goes through to Jim Broxburn's workshop.'

'She may not go through to his workshop,' I pointed out.

'Believe me, she will.'

I was aware that Keith, who always brought his cases to satisfactory conclusions, sometimes did so by methods which were entirely outwith the sanction of the law. I had in the past turned a blind eye to his misdemeanours in order to profit, on a client's behalf, from the evidence obtained, but I had no intention of becoming personally embroiled in his less reputable actions.

'Leave me out of it,' I said. 'If she happens to leave her handbag where you can get at it, I may not notice what happens next; but I am not conspiring to abet you in breaking and entering. Anyway, she'll probably come without a bag and with the keys in her pocket. Or tucked into her underwear,' I added as the horrid thought struck me. 'In that eventuality – '

'In that eventuality,' he said solemnly, 'it's up to me.'

I took some comfort from the fact that apparently I was not expected to seduce the formidable lady, nor to undress her by force. I was about to enquire whether it was not time that the police were invoked when I noticed something else.

'There's an address on that piece of brown paper,' I said.

'Mrs Chegwin's address,' said Deeley. 'I'd dearly love to picture the old besom sneaking out at night to break into dead men's homes, but the fact is that used parcel paper gets re-used and passed on. She's always handing out rhubarb to her neighbours, usually wrapped in brown paper.'

'At least it means that the would-be intruder was somebody local,' I pointed out.

'Of course it was somebody local,' Keith said impatiently. 'There was never any doubt – '

'Here she comes,' Deeley broke in. 'I'm off. If you're going to be busy, I'd better go round the traps.' He hurried away. I thought that he was as reluctant as I was to stray beyond the boundaries of what the law permitted.

'Do what you can,' Keith told me urgently. 'Play it off the cuff. When you go through to the workshop, ask her to carry something.'

'But – '

'If you want to get the lady off your back and the police off Alexander Deeley's, forget that you're a lawyer and be a devil instead.'

Mrs Farrow was approaching from the direction of Gled Corner. A light-brown bag was slung over her shoulder. She walked with an almost masculine stride which carried her briskly over the ground. She arrived in the doorway and looked at us both without either pleasure or greeting.

'Let's get on with it,' she said. 'One of you will do. You,' she said to Keith. 'You stay. I don't like anybody looking over my shoulder, but especially not lawyers.'

Keith was about to protest, but if somebody had to be cooped up with Mrs Farrow I preferred that it should

be anybody but me. 'I'll remain within call,' I said and slipped out of the door.

The heat of the day was becoming more oppressive. It would end in thunder, I thought. But Jim Broxburn's van was casting some shadow across the tractor. I spread my handkerchief over the towbar and took a seat. The day had seemed as still as death but a faint movement of air between the two vehicles made a tiny gesture towards relieving the heat. Somebody looked at me from the door of the farm manager's cottage and retired again.

How much trouble could Mrs Farrow make for me, I wondered. And for Ann Ferguson, I added guiltily. On the face of it, an unsubstantiated allegation about a will which nobody had ever seen had little chance of succeeding in court.

But suppose that she produced evidence. I did not believe that a will had ever existed, but if Mrs Farrow invented a conspiracy which also involved Alexander Deeley, then Mrs Chegwin and Mr McAngel – neither of whom had any love for Deeley and each of whom might be supposed to be her friend – might well attest to having witnessed such a will. Even if the suit did not succeed, the muck could stick. I could imagine my practice losing its highly respectable clientele and becoming the resort of those who had fraud in mind.

Could Keith really avert trouble? I put my mind to reviewing the events of the past few days, but the heat and the soporific sounds of insects conspired to defeat me. The case seemed to have grown feathers. A feather on the floor. Feathers which should have shown where the sparrowhawk had killed. Falcons. Feathers in Jim Broxburn's workshop. Feathers everywhere. I began to feel that I was smothering in feathers. I was even growing feathers. And yet, in my half-awake state, a pattern – of feathers, of course – began to emerge, faint and only

partly understood. Several of Keith's most obscure comments began to make sense, as nonsense will to a sleepy mind.

My musings were interrupted after perhaps fifteen minutes when a small ring of keys flew out of the open door and skidded to my feet. I glimpsed Keith's face mouthing something unintelligible at me.

I put my foot on the keys while I thought about it. What disaster would occur if I failed to do whatever it was that Keith wanted? What greater disaster would follow if I did as he wished?

Nobody seemed to be observing me from either the cottage or the back windows of the big house. I picked up the keys and dropped them into my pocket.

At any moment, Keith might make an excuse to come outside and change places with me. But Mrs Farrow seemed to regard me in an even more inimical light than she did Keith. She might well refuse – might already have done so. The minutes slipped by without sign of life from either cottage.

What, I wondered, did Keith expect of me? The answer was uncomfortably plain. He had intended to look inside the peel – what for, I had only a vague idea. But I was not an investigator. I might see whatever Keith wanted seen but fail to recognise it. Worse, clandestine entry to the property of others is expressly forbidden by the law which I had sworn to serve. An Englishman's home might be his castle but a Scotsman's peel was his mews . . . I pulled myself together. In the heavy heat, another light doze had been creeping up on me unsuspected.

If Keith expected me to go and look at the peel and I stayed where I was, I would never hear the last of it. There could be no harm in driving up to the vicinity. With a bit of luck Mr Farrow, or McAngel the falconer, might have returned home and I could withdraw with

my honour untainted by accusations either of turpitude or cowardice.

I got up, took a last look at the cottages and walked across the paddock. By the time I reached the car I was sweating in the now humid air. The shade had not yet reached the Rover. I drove leaning forward to avoid contact with the seat-back and with one arm out of the window to scoop cooler air into the car. Above the hills hung a blue-black raft of cloud. I willed it to come on. A good storm would clear the air and lay the dust.

At the deer-farm road, I hesitated. But I drove on. To have hidden the car would have been evidence of guilty intent, while if I had to beat a hasty retreat I preferred not to attempt it afoot. Not that I had the least intention of making an illegal entry. I parked where I had parked the previous day.

The two houses and the peel stared at me blankly. Occasional upper windows were slightly open but the doors were shut tight.

Knocking on doors would commit me to nothing and with a little luck somebody would be at home. Rehearsing in my mind what I would say in that eventuality, I realised that I was in a position to kill . . . but the metaphor about birds and stones was obviously inappropriate. If I said that I had come in the hope of seeing those fascinating birds I might even get the look inside the peel that Keith evidently craved.

With that in mind, it seemed logical to try Mr McAngel's door first. But the sound of the heavy knocker reverberated through the converted barn without waking any answering footsteps or even the bark of a dog.

I picked my way back past the peel and between the vacant perches to the house which Mrs Farrow shared with her husband. Here a more contemporary method of announcing oneself had been provided in the shape of an electric doorbell, but again I awoke no response unless you were to count a raucous cry from one of the hawks.

The keys seemed to be burning against my thigh. I looked around and listened, but the whole valley seemed to be wrapped in a Sunday calm. In that heat and humidity, no enthusiastic walkers were striding about the land. Even the cattle were seeking shade.

If the hawks belonged to Mr McAngel, Mrs Farrow might well not have a key to the peel. Keith had probably not thought of that.

Just to be sure, I decided to try a key at random in the lock of the peel. The lock was a cylinder night-latch and the most obvious key of that type was on a second ring (linked to the other) which also held a small deadlock key. I tried the first key and there was an immediate click. The door swung ponderously away from me. I would have to reach inside to pull it closed again, so it seemed foolish not to take a look.

At my intrusion and the sudden flood of light, the two hawks roused and stared haughtily at me. The room, about thirty feet by twenty, was roofed by a stone barrel-vault. The whole place had been whitewashed and was evidently kept as clean and bare as was practicable but, as Mrs Farrow had said, the soot of ages was breaking through in streaks and stains; and here and there the walls were speckled with what Keith later referred to as mutes. The floor was covered with an inch or two of clean sand, too dry to take footprints. There was a faint odour, sweet and yet acrid, like nothing that I had ever smelled before.

Set well out from the walls were perches for more than a dozen birds, hoops at one end of the room and simple posts at the other. On a hook near the door hung a single gauntlet. Otherwise the room was bare. Everything

132

was on view and all seemed to be the perfectly innocent birds and accoutrements of falconry.

I had looked inside. What more could Keith want?

In the far corner of the room, a semicircular bulge of wall intruded into the floorspace. A spiral stair, obviously, which had once led to the floors above. Leaving the outer door open for the sake of the daylight, I walked across.

A small doorway had been boarded up, very roughly, using a variety of old timbers of different colours and thicknesses and many heavy nails. I was ready to slip away. But Keith had wanted to look at something and surely there was nothing in the ground floor worth his attention – and the key to the peel had been on its own ring with another. I studied the inner doorway again. The boarding seemed to be solid and fixed. I could not see any hinges, but hinges can be concealed.

There was no handle. If the boarding was in fact a door, there must be a keyhole somewhere. I decided to spend at the most one minute in search of it before leaving with a clear conscience. The minute was more than up before I spotted it high up and near a corner, cleverly concealed behind the edge of a board thicker than the others and camouflaged by an apparently random splodge of dark paint. I tried the other key on the secondary ring. It turned. This time the whole door swung out towards me.

The doorway framed the bottom steps of a stone spiral stair, winding upward clockwise, in accordance with custom, so that in swordplay a defender would be advantaged. (Only the notorious Kerrs built their stairs going upward anti-clockwise, because they were universally left-handed. This characteristic gave rise to the expression 'caurry-fisted' which Keith had used.)

One peep, I decided, the briefest photographic glimpse, and then I would definitely go.

I went upward very cautiously. There might be nothing at the top of more significance than a dangerously disintegrating structure, but that seemed unlikely in view of the care with which the second door had been concealed. There might be no more than a cache of stolen goods. There might, on the other hand, be almost anything else from a drugs factory to a gang of bank robbers. I poked my nose cautiously over the floor above.

The upper floors were not, as Mrs Farrow had suggested, in a dangerous state and supported only by the strands of dry rot. As best I could see, the walls went up another thirty feet or more and, to judge by the pockets remaining, there had been at least two intermediate floors below the roof, but they were now non-existent, their remains entirely removed. They had been replaced by a floor (or possibly a roof) of new timber laid with some dark material, to form a shelter over most of the area, some ten or twelve feet up. The remaining strip was open to the sky.

Beneath the shelter of this new structure were more perches on which a dozen large birds were tethered. These, like their brethren below, roused and gave tongue at the sudden appearance of a human head, but their cries were different, more raucous. If their hooked beaks and glaring eyes had not marked them off for raptors I would have thought them to be gulls, for their extraordinary whiteness glowed in the dim shade. From a shrouded cube which seemed to be a cage came cries of a higher pitch.

I had no more than a nodding acquaintance with the laws pertaining to the taking and ownership of birds of prey, but the care which had been taken to hide this upper area was enough to tell me that all was not as it should be. It was very definitely time to go.

It took only a few seconds to reach that decision,

but before I could implement it I heard a voice from outside. 'Celia,' it cried. *'Celia!'* The shout seemed distant and muffled, but I was in no doubt that its owner was both perturbed and angry.

If I had moved quickly I might have been below, with the inner door relocked, before being discovered. I could then have spun a tale about finding the outer door ajar and being interested in the two birds. But rapid action is foreign to my nature and my training, leading as it so often does to bruised limbs, a pulled muscle or an impetuous error. Instead, I mounted the last few treads and stepped to one of the small arrow-slits which passed for windows.

A large, grey Range Rover was parked behind my car, completely blocking it in. I had not heard it arrive, but its driver could have spotted my car and the open door from some way off and have coasted downhill to his gate.

The man whom I presumed to have been the driver had leaned back into the vehicle, but as he straightened up again I saw that he was small and thin, looking smaller and thinner against the bulk of the big vehicle. He was casually dressed in leather boots, slacks and an open-necked shirt, but he gave the impression of being neatly pressed – all but his face, which had the hooked beak and bellicose expression of the birds around me. He moved with the nervous energy that small people often show. More than that, he had the 'lean and hungry look' that prompted Caesar to say that 'such men are dangerous'. He was certainly not McAngel, the falconer, so it had to be assumed that he was Mrs Farrow's husband. At first glance, he seemed to be a match for her in temperament if not in size. The two together would have made a formidable team. I could visualise them dominating even a meeting of angry creditors.

That was all that I had time to observe of the man before I saw that he had brought out of the Range Rover a slender gun or rifle and that he was in the process of loading something into it from a small bag slung over his shoulder. His movements, although rapid, were deft; and his handling of the weapon left me in no doubt that he was prepared to use it.

After that, I foreswore the habit of a lifetime and moved very rapidly indeed.

I descended the spiral stair a thousand times quicker than I had mounted it.

It might still have been possible to stand firm and bluff it out, but the sight of the firearm in Mr Farrow's hands and the mingled fury and determination in his face persuaded me not to stake my life on it. Instead, I hauled the inner door shut and fumbled with the key. I got the door locked not a moment too soon, because I heard him arrive in the ground floor as I backed softly around the spiral. I retreated all the way up. If he spied an empty stair through some chink in the boarding he might still think that the outer door had been left open in error and that my car belonged to some hiker who had gone up to the moors. On the other hand, he might use his gun to unlock the door, and I had no wish to be on the other side when the lock came back with all the energy which I assumed a bullet would impart to it.

A further possibility was that he had another key on him. I looked around me, but short of climbing on to a perch and pretending to be an oversized bird of prey there was nowhere to hide. The shrouded cage stood three feet off the floor and, even in the dim light beneath the false roof, only a blind man could have overlooked my legs behind the spindly metal legs supporting the cage.

I took another look out of the arrow-slit window, hoping against hope that Keith or somebody or *anybody*

136

was galloping to the rescue. I would even have settled for Sergeant Fuller, but the only person in sight was the presumed Mr Farrow. He was heading for his house with the gun still in his hands.

If he was fetching a spare key, I was doomed. I cast up my eyes to Heaven for inspiration and I found it there. If I could scramble my way on to the roof which had been built to shelter the birds, he might still find some innocent explanation to satisfy himself. There is no limit to the self-deception which people can practice, as I was demonstrating.

Evidently there was no spare key. Farrow, I saw, was returning with a large claw-hammer; so at least I had a minute or two in hand.

The stonework inside the peel was rough. Weather had eroded much of the cement; some small stones were missing altogether and occasional cracks wandered like ivy about the walls. I chose a line of ascent which would bring me up close to the edge of the roof, pushed my fingers and one toecap into such crannies as were available and began to pull myself aloft.

From below came the sound of furious hammering.

For one of my age, weight and sedentary habits the going was incredibly hard, but fear and the sound of rending timber forced me onward and upward. I pulled and hauled and scrambled until my hips were level with the edge of the roof and I was about to relieve my fingers and toes by sitting on it when I made a terrible discovery. Heaven had been jesting with me all along. The shelter over the birds was no more than a framework supporting some sort of tarred paper which would not have supported the weight of a cat, let alone that of a plumpish solicitor weighed down with years.

I hooked one buttock on to the edge and rested my fingers while I thought about it. I might perhaps have managed to walk across the framework; but that refuge seemed much less attractive now that I knew how insubstantial a barrier it would place between me and whatever was in the gun.

Looking upward again I realised that Heaven, possibly mistaking me for someone younger and more agile, had been right all along. The one place where I might escape observation, or at least be relatively safe from gunfire, would be on the very top of the walls.

I wasted a few more seconds trying to spot some less demanding avenue of escape, but the sound of a violent assault on the door below me suggested that time was running out. I pushed my tender fingers into the nearest joint in the stonework and began to climb again.

If somebody had that morning suggested that I could climb straight up about forty feet of vertical stonework, I would have laughed him to scorn. But desperation can lend a man a strength which he had thought had vanished over the horizon of time. Ignoring pain, exhaustion and the damage to my suit and toecaps, I forced myself upward.

The higher I climbed, the more the weather had eroded the joints in the stonework. Hand- and footholds became better and more frequent. But, to offset this advantage, I was tiring rapidly, while the drop below me seemed to add a weight of its own to mine. A pigeon which had been nesting in one of the arrow-slits clattered out, nearly dislodging me. I hung on somehow, with my nose over an untidy nest holding two pale eggs, until my heart slowed down to a mad pounding.

My fingertips were in agony and my muscles burned. They would not support me for much longer. I went up the last few feet in a desperate scramble. Below me, I heard the unmistakable sound of the door being reduced to matchwood.

To get first my elbows and then my stomach on to the very summit of the stonework was at first a huge relief and all that I could do was to hang there, gasping and looking at the world. The black screen of cloud had advanced and was now almost overhead. Below me, the grass seemed a mile away but I was not seriously aware of the drop until a bird, another pigeon I think, flew past below me. Then the empty void, before and behind, reached up to grab at me.

The walls, which had been more than four feet thick at the bottom doorway, must have tapered, because they were little more than the width of my body at their top. Teetering on what seemed to be a knife-edge above an abyss, I managed to swivel myself around until I was lying along the top of the wall. And as I did so, the last of my confidence was shattered by two more blows. A blast of wind came suddenly below the cloud, almost carrying me away. And beneath me I heard a grating sound and felt the stones move slightly in their ancient beds. They steadied again, but the impression that the entire tower was about to crumble remained, paramount over all my other fears. I closed my eyes, clung tight to the unstable wallhead and tried to resemble one of the many bulges in the stonework.

From far below, I heard feet on the spiral staircase and a cry from one of the falcons. My eyes refused to open and the wind which was plucking at my clothes also filled my ears, but I could picture him glaring around for the intruder. Emanations of hostility seemed to fill the tower and wash over me, leaving a stain behind.

My perch felt too precarious to allow of any movement. Some part of me must be showing over the edge but not, I sincerely hoped, any vital organs. I concentrated on hugging the stones, determined not to fall even if a bullet or a load of shot punctured my periphery. I was more afraid of the drop than of any weapon. I could survive pain, but not a fall.

Minutes passed and nothing happened. I clung on, whipped by the wind. The world stabilised a little and I managed to crack one eye open. I looked first down into the interior of the tower because the drop was less on that side and the false roof made it seem even shorter. If the man was there, he must be under the false roof.

Greatly daring, I conquered vertigo and looked at my left, down on the outside world. I was becoming acclimatised to the height, for the conviction that I was stationary while the world revolved around me was less than before. I saw him then and knew that I was in even more trouble. He was backing away across the grass and looking up towards me. For a moment, I thought that our eyes met. He whipped the gun to his shoulder.

Keith, no doubt, would have recognised the gun and have made mental calculations about trajectories. That was how his mind worked. I only knew that terrible things were going to happen but that if I could only survive I could endure. I cringed away and the stones groaned again beneath me.

The shot, when it came, sounded less loud than I had expected. Something hit the stonework below me and whirred high into the wind. It landed on the grass. He walked over and picked it up and then threw it aside. It seemed to be a metal object with a tuft of something coloured at one end. He dipped into the bag at his side and began to reload the gun. It must have been a complicated operation because it took him most of a minute.

His second shot sent something whizzing low over my head. He loaded again and began to back away. From his low viewpoint I thought that he could see no more than a thin slice of my body with a hump at hip and shoulder. The ground fell slightly and I thought – and hoped – that whatever he gained in an improved view of his target he would lose in the increasing range.

The third shot again hit stone. The missile rebounded and hung for a tantalising second in the air before falling away.

The Farrow conjugal residence presented a blank gable to me, but from my precarious perch I was looking almost into an upper window of McAngel's house, some forty yards off. It stared back at me. From there, he would have an easy shot. Farrow, I thought, might or might not have a key to the other man's house.

His mind, it seemed, was following a parallel track. Registering anger and frustration, even in plan view, by virtue of the rigid set of his head and shoulders, he vanished from my view around the corner of the peel. I closed my eyes for a blissful minute of fantasising that I was safe at home. McAngel seemed to be fussy about locking up. This would be the wrong day for him to have left an accessible window open.

He had not been so careless. Above the wind I heard the gutteral cry of one of the birds and I looked down to my right, to see the man appear suddenly out of the spiral staircase.

For the first time, he addressed me directly. 'Are you coming down?' he yelled at me. 'Or do I have to come up there and push you off?'

There seemed to be no point in answering. Even had I been willing to descend and confront him I knew that I could never climb down unaided. Insecure as my roost might be, I preferred to remain where I was; and if he climbed up to dislodge me I made up my mind that I would take him and half the wall with me. In the meantime, any seconds which he spent awaiting my answer might be seconds added to my lifespan.

'Right, you bastard!' he shouted up at me.

He laid the gun down carefully and threaded a stick from the shattered boarding through the back of his belt. Evidently his intention was to poke me off the wall from a safe distance. He came to the wall below me, studied the handholds and began to climb.

I could wait and try to kick him off as he arrived. But there was only fear to anchor me where I was. By the time he arrived, I could be at the other end of the building. As a practising coward I preferred the latter option.

Bringing my hands and toes up to the edges of the wallhead, I commanded them to push me along; but they refused to lessen the frail stability which I had managed to achieve. I made an effort of will and began to lift my weight off my body.

Without warning, two large stones under my right hand began to pivot and slide. Only the grip of my other hand and a convulsive jerk of my left leg out into space saved me from falling. The stones went. Hanging head down over the void, I watched them dwindle in perspective. The man tried to leap clear, but he was too late. The larger stone wiped him off the wall and smashed him down on to the sandstrewn stone floor. He moved and his limbs twitched but I knew that he was dead. From the captive birds came a chorus of savage cries – not of distress but of exultation. Death was a familiar friend to them.

The fall of the stones and the man's death brought back my vertigo with interest. Despite the missing stones where my right arm had been, I managed to give myself back some sort of equilibrium. My legs clamped on to the wall as if it had been a horse, my hands clutched the remaining stones and I think that I tried to find a grip with my teeth.

Only seconds later, it seemed, the storm arrived. The

heavens opened and a torrent of water fell on my back and bounced off the stonework before my face. I was soaked to the skin within seconds, but I was prepared to tolerate the added discomfort. I was alive and still as fast to my perch as the falcons below were to theirs. That was enough for the moment.

NINE

A womblike inertia took hold of me. My body was still clamped to the stonework but my mind was numb. It might have been a minute or an hour later that I was roused by the sound of another vehicle approaching. Dear God, let it not be another enemy! I could not survive again. I opened an eye and turned my head slowly. Keith's jeep was emerging from the sheets of rain. I let my eye close. The worst was over. Keith would know what to do. He would magic me down to safety.

The jeep's door slammed and I heard Keith's voice. 'Anyone at home?' he called and then, 'Ralph?'

'Here,' I shouted. Even that tiny movement threatened to topple me.

'Where's here?'

'Look up,' I called – very gently, but I felt a minute shift in the stones beneath me.

Keith wasted no words on pointless questions or exclamations of surprise. He came straight to the point. 'Can you get down?'

'No,' I said. Again that small tremor.

'Hang on.'

I was alone with the wind and the rain for a full minute. Then I heard Keith arrive in the room below me. He seemed unsurprised by the secret space and the strange, white birds, nor yet by the crushed body. 'Throw me down Mrs Farrow's keys,' he called.

In which pocket had I put them? I thought back. Right-hand jacket. Very gently, trying hard not to move a muscle outside my right arm, I moved, felt for the keys. My jacket had twisted around me and the wet cloth obstructed my efforts, but I found the keys and dropped them down to Keith.

I was alone again but the wind was dropping and I thought that the rain was diminishing.

Keith's voice was back. 'Help will be here soon,' he said. 'Are you safe until it arrives?'

'I don't know,' I said.

Something in my voice must have told him that I was at the end of my tether. 'Hang on,' he said. 'I'm coming up.'

'No,' I said. 'These stones are loose.'

'I'll be careful.'

I could hear faint sounds and the falling of rotten mortar as he climbed towards me. 'Much virtue in the rock-climbing I did in my youth,' his voice said suddenly, almost in my ear. I opened my eyes in surprise, to see him finish a careful testing of the stones and then roll gently on to the wallhead facing me. He reached out his hands. 'Grab hold,' he said. 'I won't let you fall. Three more stones are loose but they have an adequate bed. They won't fall unless you do something athletic.'

I shifted carefully and took his hands. They were slippery with the wet, but their grip was infinitely comforting. I could almost believe that if I slipped he would catch me. I found that I could speak without a sensation of imminent doom.

'Rock-climbing my eye,' I said faintly. 'Bedroom-window-climbing more likely.'

'You could be right. I phoned the police and the fire

146

brigade from Mrs Farrow's phone. I don't know why you climbed up but I can quite see why you couldn't climb down. I'm not looking forward to making the descent myself.'

I was feeling braver now that I was no longer alone. 'I hope you left the money for the calls. Where is the lady?'

'Emergency calls are free,' he said. 'Anyway, she owes us. She's just given herself away as having been, at the very least, an accessory after the fact of Jim Broxburn's murder. I left her locked in the keeper's store. What on earth induced you to come up here on your own?'

'You threw the keys out but you didn't follow. I thought that she'd refused to be parted from your bonny blue eyes. I knew that you wanted to look inside the peel. I guessed that you were leaving it to me.'

I could feel his suppressed laughter through our clenched fingers. It seemed to rock the whole wall. 'You're a rotten guesser,' he said. 'I wanted you to hang on to the keys in case she spotted that they were gone and insisted that I turn out my pockets. But I was too interested in watching her search desperately for the two things you've got in that envelope to leave just then. When I realised that you were no longer with us, I came after you as fast as I could.'

'I don't call this very fast,' I said. 'I've been stuck here for hours.'

'It's not much over an hour since we parted company,' Keith said.

'It felt like a year. I suppose it'll be as long again before the brigade arrives with ladders?'

Before he could answer there was a sudden groan from the wall. The stones shifted under me and I heard a smaller one fall. From the muffled sound of it I thought that it must have landed on the body, but I preferred neither to look nor ask.

I felt Keith's grip tighten. 'Keep still,' he said.

'I am keeping still.'

'No you're not. You twitched. Take your mind off it. Have you worked out yet what's been happening?'

'Some of it. Most of it, I think.'

'Tell me. Perhaps I can fill in some gaps for you. You may even be able to fill some for me.'

My mind wanted to think about the stability of the wall and how on earth anybody was going to get me down from it. A helicopter seemed to be called for, but I would have settled for a large crane. Keith's philosophy, I knew, was 'If you can't do anything about it, ignore it.' I decided that his attitude made more sense than mine did. With a great effort, I laid my cheek down on a stone and concentrated on the recent past rather than on the immediate future.

It took me a few seconds to find a starting point. 'I suppose that that was Mr Farrow,' I said. 'I think that he was shooting at me with tranquilliser darts. That's how he killed Jim Broxburn. And you knew it all along,' I added severely. 'That's why you asked Fergus about the shotguns.'

'That's right. A Conservator dart-gun. It looks very like a four-ten shotgun. I knew that he had something of the sort, because they use them around a deer farm.'

'I suppose you sold it to him?'

'No,' he said. I was about to apologise for suspecting him of taking an unfair advantage in the deduction stakes when he went on. 'I ordered it from Liverpool and sold it to the slaughterhouse. They sometimes had a large bullock take a dislike to the idea of being turned into beef and break loose; and the police have an equal dislike of rifles being used in the streets of the town.

'I wondered what had happened to it after the

148

slaughterhouse closed. The deer farm must have bought it. I don't know much about Farrow, but I remember that he had his firearms certificate taken off him some years ago because that temper of his got him into trouble. There's no way the police will let him own a firearm again. His partner has to be the certificate holder, but I've met him in the shop and he's a nervous character who knows damn-all about firearms. Farrow has to have been the user. You were lucky that he missed you; the Conservator is more accurate than most dart-guns.'

I kept still, doubting whether the wall would withstand a good shiver. 'I suppose it was loaded with tranquilliser this time,' I said.

'Bound to be. He wouldn't be carrying alpha-chloralose around with him.'

'That's what I thought. But he loaded a dart with rat-poison for Jim Broxburn's benefit.' As the words left my mouth I realised more. 'You suspected that all along. Penny said that you picked up a cartridge which was either two-two or from a dummy launcher.'

'Full marks to Penny. The Conservator uses a crimped two-two Long Rifle cartridge, very like the blank used in a launcher,' Keith said. 'And then I knew that I was right from the moment I saw Mrs Chegwin's photographs. The puncture wound looked too big to have been made by the small syringe that was found near the body. The needle on a dart intended to be shot into a deer has to be much thicker.'

That took me by surprise. 'I thought that it looked about right,' I said.

'That's what was wrong with it. A puncture wound in skin partly closes up again as soon as whatever made it is withdrawn. The pathologist probably said as much but your Sergeant preferred to disregard it.'

I nodded, very gently, while thinking hard thoughts

149

about the Sergeant. 'So Farrow went after Jim Broxburn, taking with him the dart-gun, a supply of rat-poison and a dead pheasant,' I said. 'That makes it premeditated. He shot him in the hand with the dart. And then what? I suppose he apologised profusely for the unfortunate accident. Broxburn thought that he'd only been tranquillised and allowed himself to be helped towards home, where he could sleep it off or get medical help. When he collapsed and died, Farrow set up the faked accident.'

It was Keith's turn to pause for thought. 'I'll go along with that,' he said at last. 'It's as good a scenario as we're likely to get, unless the widow cares to talk. And when I last saw her, she was confining her remarks to calling me names. Have you worked out yet why Jim Broxburn was killed? And why you nearly followed the same road?'

'There are three possibilities,' I said. 'The jealous husband. Or belief in the legacy. Or a third . . . '

'Or a combination of all three,' Keith said. 'Go on. What's the third?'

'The last cutting in Jim Broxburn's scrapbook,' I said, 'was about a black market in birds of prey. Hawks and falcons – or are they the same thing?'

'Different. Hawks are short-winged, falcons have long wings. Sparrowhawks. Peregrine falcons. You saw one of each in the ground floor. McAngel keeps both so, to be pedantic, when he's flying a falcon he's a falconer; with a hawk, he's an austringer. You're right again,' Keith said. 'The black market has sagged in the last couple of years, but you can still get a whale of a price for the right goods if you can get them to Germany, which is the market centre.'

I began to nod again but I stopped myself. I had almost forgotten for the moment the inner voice which said that it would only take a nod to start the collapse of the whole building. 'That room below us is intended

150

to be secret. There's something surreptitious going on, but I don't know enough to figure out any details. You'd better tell me the rest.'

The wind had faded to a modest breeze and the rain was only a thin drizzle. Below us, the chicks began to cry *kee-kee* and the older birds joined in with their hoarser cry. 'Feeding time,' Keith said as the noise died down. 'They sound as if they have sore throats. I can tell you a lot more but some of it, I admit, is because I phoned a big wheel in the British Falconry Society last night.'

'When did you catch on?' I asked him.

'Slowly. You'd have caught on if you'd had a chance to look at what you've got in your pocket,' he said generously. 'I was intrigued when you mentioned the white feathers in Jim Broxburn's box in the workshop.'

'I thought that he kept them for fly-tying,' I said.

'White's almost never used for artificial flies. And then a feather from a peregrine falcon turned up – again in the cottage.'

It was a struggle but I was almost keeping up with him. 'Which is the peregrine falcon?' I asked.

'The one with the yellow feet on the block perch. Didn't you notice the barred legs? The feather Mrs Ferguson spotted made me think of those legs. That suggested that somebody from here had tried to search the cottage. So when we came to visit Mrs Farrow yesterday, I kept my eyes and ears open. By pure chance, we picked a day when McAngel was away with most of his birds and the two he'd left behind were out on the grass; yet I was sure that I heard the sound of a falcon from somewhere inside the peel. Otherwise it would have been the perfect hiding place. Any noise would be put down to McAngel's hawks and falcons; and the legend that the peel was full of collapsing floors would have kept curious visitors away.

'So I did some telephoning last night. I wanted to know

151

about McAngel, but his reputation is whiter than white. He'll certainly say that he knew nothing about what went on in the upper floor. It could even be true. Mrs Farrow did all the real work, remember, and McAngel must be a wee bit deaf – did you notice how Alec Deeley raised his voice when he spoke to him?

'But when I probed a bit more, I learned a lot about Mr Farrow. And a lot that I didn't know about falcons. Most of the big money paid for falcons comes from the Middle East. Gyrfalcons are favoured, but above all they fancy the white Arctic falcon. It's quite a rarity. Occasionally a pair find their way down into the Highlands from Greenland and decide to stick around. But the white coloration soon gets diluted as they interbreed with native gyrfalcons.'

'Those are pure-bred, white Arctic falcons below us?' I asked.

'That's just what they are. And any sheik would swap his favourite concubine for one of them. I don't suppose a couple of them would be missed,' Keith added thoughtfully. 'You know the law about birds of prey?'

I had done some superficial reading into the subject two days earlier. 'Under the Wildlife and Countryside Act,' I said, 'it's illegal to take raptors in the wild. The Secretary of State, through the Department of the Environment, can issue licences to allow them to be taken in the wild or imported; and all captive hawks and falcons must be ringed and registered with the D. of E. I take it that he hasn't issued Mr Farrow with any licences?'

'That he has not,' Keith said. 'Seven or eight years ago, two pairs of white Arctic falcons were spotted nesting in a remote glen up in Sutherland, but before anybody could organise a watch the whole lot vanished. The chicks would be easy but God knows how he managed to get the adult birds.'

152

'Tranquilliser darts?' I suggested. My mind was running on them at the time.

'Possibly, although I don't know of them ever being used on birds of prey. Tranquillisers take time to work and the bird would certainly panic and take off. It could conk out in mid-air and kill itself in the fall. Drugged bait would be almost as risky but it's possible. He'd have been hard pressed to use cage-traps or leg-traps in the time available.

'Anyway – surprise, surprise! – a few weeks later a Mr Farrow made application to the D. of E. for a licence to import Arctic falcons. The coincidence was a bit much for even a civil servant to swallow. The phone lines grew hot and Mr Farrow was visited where he then lived, near Kelso. Nothing was found, but Farrow was told unofficially that he would never be granted a licence to own as much as a kestrel and that if he was ever found in possession of a bird of prey he was for it. And the penalties are stiff.

'Not long after, he bought the peel and the adjoining house and gave McAngel the use of the ground floor of the peel. I suspect that Mrs Chegwin was asked by the RSPB to keep an eye on him, but she was more interested in pursuing her feud with Alec Deeley. Farrow must have been breeding Arctic falcons in captivity ever since and getting them smuggled to Germany. As an exporter of venison he must have made friends in shipping circles. Your turn.'

'Not really,' I said, 'because you aren't playing fair. You know what Mrs Farrow was looking for. But I'll make a guess. Jim Broxburn, on one of his visits to her, found white feathers on the grass. Those are the feathers I found in the workshop.'

'Correct. Of course, the white feathers could have come from a gull or a dove, but found outside a falconer's mews

153

they started him wondering. Very probably he had heard rumours of the old scandal. When he wrote to his sister, he enclosed a note to her husband with one of the feathers, asking him to get it identified. And with her next letter she enclosed her husband's reply to the effect that, according to his friend in the Biology Department, the feather had come from a member of the falcon family and the white colour suggested the Arctic falcon. The police have that letter now, but she phoned her husband for confirmation.'

Much was becoming clear, but one or two areas remained obscure. 'How did they know that Jim Broxburn had found out and was preparing to do something about it?'

'I'd be guessing.'

'Guess, then.'

'Pillow talk. He stayed off his work on Monday night, so you said, and we may find that Farrow was away from home. Perhaps Broxburn asked one question too many and let out that he knew too much. You've seen what a hard nut Mrs Farrow can be.'

'They don't come much harder,' I said.

'Perhaps she backed him into a corner. He may have had to put his cards on the table. The two attempts to sneak into his cottage, and Mrs Farrow's determination to look through his effects, show that they had some idea of what evidence he was holding. And now,' Keith said, 'the rain has stopped, the sun looks like coming out and your ordeal is almost over. Here comes the fire brigade.'

With my eyes tight shut, I had become absorbed in our talk. As the facts surrounding Jim Broxburn's demise became clearer, part of my mind had begun to wonder whether our theory could be proved. Mr Farrow's death would be the subject of a Fatal Accident Enquiry and my testimony, together with the existence of the birds,

154

the feathers and the dart-gun, would go a long way towards incriminating him and clearing the names of Jim Broxburn and Alexander Deeley. If Farrow's widow were to be prosecuted as an accomplice, which seemed probable, the higher level of proof required . . .

The discomfort of my position had become no more than a fact of life and I had forgotten for the moment the drop over which we were balanced. At Keith's words I was jerked back from a mental appraisal of the evidence. A return of vertigo made my head spin. The noise of the fire appliance seemed to be a mile below us.

Keith felt my sudden clutch at his hands. 'It's all right,' he said. 'They'll soon get us down. And then we'd better be prepared to answer questions. There's a car following the fire engine and I think it belongs to Sergeant Fuller.'

'How?' I said. 'How will they get us down?'

'You have a point. I don't think they can get close enough to use the turntable ladder. Hold on to the stonework a minute.'

I transferred my grip to the stones and felt them shift minutely as he tested their stability. 'H'm,' he said.

To keep my mind occupied with less awesome matters, I turned it towards the story we would have to tell. 'You still have Mrs Farrow's keys,' I reminded him.

He caught the direction of my thoughts immediately. 'Yes. You found both doors open.'

'Then why did he have to break down the inner door?'

'H'm. Got it!' Keith said triumphantly. 'You found Mrs Farrow's keys in it. That's how you came to find the hidden lock. When he threatened you, you locked the inner door after you. She may deny leaving her keys behind, but who's going to believe her? I robbed a chicken for some white feathers to put in Jim Broxburn's workshop, and found them again in her

155

bag in the presence of Deeley and several of his working party.'

That seemed to provide what one client of mine, a chemist by profession, had called a satisfactory allotrope of the truth. I allowed my mind to return to the more important matter. 'I don't think that I could climb on to a ladder. My joints seem to have locked up.'

The fire engine had stopped beyond the wall. I heard the fire officer's voice calling some questions.

'This wall's unstable,' Keith called back. 'Several stones are on the point of falling inwards. It won't support a ladder. You'd better get out a canvas.'

'I can't jump into a blanket,' I said quickly.

'Stop thinking about it,' he said. He gripped my wrists again, at the same time handing me the bunch of keys. 'Listen to me and let your brain drift along. You're lying beside a swimming pool. You're wearing swimming trunks and the sun's hot on your back.'

I could feel the real sun on my neck and see a glow through my eyelids. Evidently the storm had passed. 'Yes,' I said.

'You can hear children laughing and the splash as somebody goes off the diving board.'

His voice droned on, hypnotically factual, describing the scene. He was buying time, I suppose, while the firemen spread the canvas and got into position. Soon the pool was very real to me.

'You're hot,' Keith said at last. 'But you feel too stiff and lazy to get up. The cool water is to your left and just a foot or two below you. Penny's in the water and calling to you. Just roll off and you can have a lovely swim. Lift up your right leg.'

'I can't lift it,' I said. The hip-joint was aching fiercely.

'You must. Try hard. The cool water's waiting for you.'

I flexed my leg, managed to hook my toe on to the

156

wall and began straightening my knee. 'That'll do,' Keith said. 'Dip your toe in the water. Have a lovely swim.'

As I reached down with my left leg he lifted my right hand suddenly and I found myself falling. By then, I was more than half expecting to hit water; but before I had time for fear to return I landed flat on my back and bounced once, twice. The ring of firemen lowered the canvas to the ground. I had doubts as to whether I would ever be able to walk again, but I was pulled to my feet and hustled away from the wall. The sun was shining and the band of black cloud was moving away in the general direction of England. Beside my foot lay a battered metal dart.

'Come on down,' I called up to Keith. 'It's a doodle.'

'Not on your life,' he replied. 'I'm coming down the easy way.' He disappeared from sight and began the long climb down.

Sergeant Fuller closed in.